Baird: Encouraged to Trust

The Barnabas Chronicles
Book 1

By

Ronna M. Bacon

Joshua 1:9

Have I not commanded you? Be strong and of good courage; do not be afraid, nor be dismayed, for the Lord your God is with you wherever you go. (NJKV)

Table of Contents

The fallen crisp leaves crunched under his feet as Baird Cassidy shuffled around the perimeter of the enclosed yard, the high board fence preventing him from seeing what lay beyond his prison. And prison it was, even though he had been allowed out that day, day three, he thought.

He had awakened in a rough cell two days earlier, his head pounding as he felt the lump under the tousled waves of dark brown hair, his light hazel eyes squinting against the meagre light coming in through the dirty windows. He had rolled to his side, fighting the nausea that roiled in his stomach. He had finally pushed himself upright, his legs swinging over the edge of the bunk he had apparently just been dumped on, no blanket to cover him against the chill.

He stood, his hand reaching to steady himself against the rough stone, his head spinning for a moment, before he made his way around the small room, finding the windows and then the door. He had shaken the door, eventually banging on it, without rousing anyone. He had slumped back on the bunk, his head drooping before he flopped over on his side, losing the fight to keep himself awake. He didn't hear the quiet whispers of sound as the critters that shared his room crept out and observed him before scurrying away, knowing they would find no food there. Not yet.

He was roused by the hands that shook him roughly and then hauled him to his feet, hands gripping his arms shoving him forward, his feet stumbling over each other until he gained enough balance to walk on his own. He was thrust down into a chair, a bowl of soup set in front of him, and ordered to eat. That was all he would get that day, he was told. He finally nodded, his eyes slipping open and closed as he picked up the spoon and began to eat.

The scene was repeated the next two days, but on the third day of his captivity, he got a glimpse of a woman, no, lady, he thought as she moved silently around the room, not looking at anything but what she was working on. He watched through lowered eyelashes as he ate as slowly as he could, taking in her tousled, unkempt black hair, the thinness of her face and arms, what he could see of them. He saw the bruises on her arms and grew angry and then sighed. Lord, what have I gotten involved in? We were sent out, what three days ago, four, told to find a certain house and that we needed to find the thumb drives and packages left for our boss, Barnabas? That went well until we were on the way back to our vehicles and we were ambushed. I don't remember what happened. Lord, let the other five on my team have made it out. Please, Lord? I don't care about me, but don't let them have been hurt.

Berneen Dakin tried hard to watch the man that had been brought to the prison, or whatever it was that she was kept in, without it being obvious. She had no idea who he was, but she prayed he made it out alive. He was not the first one brought there. But any of the others had lasted only a few days and then disappeared. When she had first asked about them, the blows from the leader's hands had sent her to the floor, a huddled heap. She had pulled herself up after a while and dragged herself to the room next to the jail cell, the dampness and chill of it a welcome respite from the coarse voices and even coarser words she had to endure when she was on the main floor of the building. She spent as little time there as she could, seeking refuge and protection in her room, the door locking on the inside.

She watched from the corner of her eye that day as the man ate and then was roughly handled and shoved through the door to the backyard. He would be only allowed out there for thirty minutes, less if he tried to escape. That she knew. She looked around, her tasks done for the day, and then she too slipped through the door, shrinking back into a corner, knowing she could not be seen. Some of the guards would punish her for being out there, that she knew, but the one who was there that day, wouldn't. He seemed kinder than the others, but she didn't trust him. She had lost her trust in people, having been imprisoned in this place for two months, she thought. Three, perhaps? God had abandoned her, that she had decided. She had prayed for release but none had come.

Her face raised to the sun, she closed her eyes, relishing the few moments of freedom she would have. She would be dragged back in soon, meals to prepare, laundry to do, the building to clean. She despaired of ever getting free. Her gaze shot around as she heard a whisper of a sound, not sure what it was. Her gaze landed on the other prisoner, watching as he turned, his head tilted, trying to determine, she thought, what the sound was and where it came from.

The guard moved towards Baird, his hand out to shove him towards the building when Baird's fist flew towards his jaw, knocking him down and out. Baird watched as his team mates, or some of them, appeared at the top of the fence, dropping down near him, their voices muted as they approached.

"Baird, come. We need to leave now." His team leader, Branigan Clery, was at his side, pushing him towards the wall, not understanding why Baird hesitated, his eyes on the building.

Then, Baird saw her, huddled in the corner, her hands covering her mouth. "Branigan, we need to take her with us."

"Take who?" Branigan swung, his eyes meeting those of Berneen, before one of the other men was at her side, tugging her towards Baird, even as she fought him, struggling to free her arm, dragging herself backwards, her feet digging into the ground, her long hair flying loose around her, fear on her face.

Blair Campion finally just swept her into his arms and ran for the wall, handing her up and over and then scaling the wall, dropping lightly beside her, watching closely as Baird reached for her hand and pulled her with him. His eyes dropped to her feet and then he was beside Baird.

"She has no shoes on, Baird!"

"What!" Baird slid to a halt, his eyes on Blair before he stared at Berneen, finally dropping his gaze to her bare feet. He mumbled something and simply swept her into his arms, a small cry coming from her before her arms were around his neck.

—

They heard the yells of outrage from behind the walls and quickened their pace, finding the vehicle they had hidden, leaving Brady Coghlan behind the wheel. Once they were all inside, he sped away, not caring that he was driving over the speed limit.

Baird dropped to a seat, his breath in gasps, his head pounding afresh, his eyes sliding closed for a moment before they popped open, his gaze finding furious gray eyes that had flecks of blue, green, and amber in them glaring at him.

His hand went up, even as Blair spoke.

"Miss? Cut the anger. We couldn't leave you there."

She spun in her seat, her glare directed at Blair. "You have no idea what you just did. I can't leave there." She struggled to reach for the door, her hands clasped gently but tightly in Baird's. "Please, I need to go back."

"We can't let you. Why is it so important that you do?"

"They'll kill someone close to me. They threatened that already." She slumped back, her hands, freed from Baird's grasp at her words, covering her face even as sobs shook her body.

"Miss, we'll make sure they're safe. Let me know the names."

She shook her head. "I can't. They're in hiding and I can't send anyone to them."

She sank back further, Baird's eyes on her before sudden pain in his head caused a groan to be torn from his body and he collapsed, a hand reaching for her, even as she turned, fear on her face.

"They hurt him, didn't they?"

Blair nodded, his eyes exchanging glances with the men even as he reached for Baird, easing him back on the seat, seeing Berneen reaching to cradle him, a shuttered look covering her face.

"Do you know who did this?" Blair's voice was stern, matching the look on his face.

She nodded. "I think I do. He's vicious. I prayed to get away but couldn't. He'll be beyond furious that this man escaped. They never do. I think, if you look, you'll find graves around the walls. Men would be there and then just disappear." She sounded defeated, drawing the attention of the five men to her before their eyes dropped to Baird, wondering just how close it had been for him.

Chapter 2

Baird was carried carefully to the infirmary on the first floor of the main building in their headquarters compound and gently laid on a hospital bed, and Brady had then disappeared, on the hunt for Doc Whitson. The men that had carried him in stood back, their eyes watchful, hurting for their comrade, even as Blair had carried Berneen in and set her on a bed in a neighbouring room, despite her protests. He had to physically restrain her from fleeing the room, finally standing in the doorway, arms crossed, a frown on his face as he watched her pace. He could not understand her attitude. His head turned as he heard footsteps and saw the physician heading his way, stopping at Baird's room.

He turned back, to find Berneen in front of him, her arms wrapped around herself.

"How is he?" She had an unreadable look on her face, but her eyes showed her concern. Those she could not shutter, no matter how much she wanted to.

"Baird?" At her nod, he just shook his head. "Doc's with him now. We'll see what he has to say. But we need to do something about you."

She snorted, spun and walked away, leaving him staring after her in disbelief. He stepped back from the doorway in the hall as he heard his name called and Breck Curran walked his way. Breck was over the two

—

teams of men, reporting directly to their employer, Barnabas Carey.

"Blair? Talk to me. What's going on?"

Blair simply shook his head. "We found Baird, tried to get him out, and he insisted the lady imprisoned there as well just had to come with us."

"Lady? We had no reports on a female there." Breck watched over Blair's shoulder for a moment. "She needs someone to take care of her."

"She does. I asked Anna to come over."

Breck nodded. "Good. Have Doc take a look at her." He paused, a thoughtful look on his face. "Do we have a name?"

"Not yet. She has not been exactly cooperative with us. In fact, she has been hostile, not happy that we removed her as well. She stated that she had someone close to her that had been threatened with death but refused to tell us who or where they are."

The two men looked around as they heard brisk steps on the wooden hallway floor and saw Anna Whitson headed their way, stopping first to check on Baird before she appeared in front of them. Anna mothered all, Blair thought, and then sighed. She was Barnabas' housekeeper, had been housekeeper to his parents until they retired, when they told Anna they were buying a small condo and that she could retire. She had snorted, simply held out her hand for a key and showed up at their condo once a week to clean. She took interest in all the men employed by Barnabas, including Barnabas, shaking her head at the fact that he had hired only men who were single, orphans, and had the same initials as his. She had stared at him at first, but then informed him that that would never last. These educated men, as she termed them, would never stay with him.

She had been proven wrong, a loyalty to Barnabas burning within each one. She prayed daily for her boys, as she called them, and for life mates for them.

She looked up at Breck and then Blair, before she stood where she could watch Berneen.

"What's her story, Blair?"

"We have no idea. Baird refused to leave the place without her. She's not happy about that, says someone close to her has been threatened with death. And no, we have not been able to find out her name."

Anna nodded, before she turned. "I'll be right back. Sarah left some clothes that I think will fit her. I know my slippers will. She can't be walking around at this time of year in her bare feet."

She was back in no time, dropping the clothing on the bed, and then turning to find Berneen. Berneen had dropped into a corner, her arms around her knees, her face buried. Anna's heart broke for the young woman but knew she had to get her up and on her feet, showered, hair shampooed, and dressed in clothes that were clean.

She stood in front of Berneen for a moment, her eyes assessing the younger woman, seeing the neglect

—

15

and abuse that she had undergone, subtle signs that the men would have missed.

"Young lady, let's get you on your feet." Anna's voice was soft but firm. She watched as Berneen ignored her. She reached down at that point, a hand grasping Berneen's arm gently.

Berneen flinched, her arms going up to cover her head. Anna heard an exclamation from the two men, who moved towards her, stopping as she raised a hand and shook her head.

"Come on, dear. On your feet. I think you would like to get cleaned up and into some clean clothes. Doc wants to check you over but I asked him to wait until you had a chance to have a shower or a bath, whichever you prefer."

Berneen lowered her arms, her gaze finding the kindly one of the older woman and frowned. "I can't. I'm not allowed."

Anna heard the low growls from the two men and waved them back. "Well, I have no idea who told you that. But that person is not here and not in charge of you anymore. You're here visiting me and I know after travelling I always like to get washed and into clean clothes." She gently drew Berneen to her feet and, an arm around her, led her over to the bed. "My granddaughter's about your size. These will do until we can get you your own clothes. Now, pick out what you want and I'll take you somewhere you can clean up."

Berneen reached out a tentative finger at last, touching the clothing, tears near the surface. Anna gave a sound and then swept the younger woman into her arms, holding her as she wept. Berneen finally moved back, wiping at her eyes.

"Thank you."

"And we do need to know your name. We can't continue to call you by the names we have been, although they all suit you."

"Berneen." That was all Berneen was able to get out, overcome with emotions. At Anna's questioning look, she spelt it out for her.

"Berneen! A lovely name for a lovely young lady. But you must have two names, as my grandson would say."

Berneen looked up at the ceiling, blinking past the tears, knowing that once she gave her name, she was losing her anonymity and that anyone searching her name would find the one she was trying so hard to protect.

"It's Dakin. I'm Berneen Dakin."

"Beautiful names for a beautiful lady. Now, pick what you want and I'll show you the guest room where you can clean up. Doc will want you back here to look you over, make sure you're not harmed, but he's in no rush."

"But he has to be." Berneen rushed to pick up the first outfit she touched.

Blair spoke from beside her, causing her to jump, fear on her face as she turned to him.

"Anna's right. Take your time." He nodded at the clothing. "Pick what you want to wear, not what you think you should, or the first thing you touch. Doc's in no rush. He's still with Baird, and then he muttered something about a piece of apple pie with his name on it." He grinned at Anna. "I just want to know it there's one with your name on it."

Anna laughed, even as she turned him around and shooed him from the room. "Those boys! Always hungry and always teasing! But they have hearts of gold, every single one of them."

Thirty minutes later, Anna tucked Berneen into the bed in the infirmary room. Berneen had hardly been able to stay awake, feeling clean for the first time in months, she realized, her hair washed and braided. She snuggled down under the blankets, relishing the warmth and feeling with her sock-covered feet the hot water bottle Anna had tucked in the bottom of the bed. She had finally chosen a long-sleeved T-shirt and leggings, feeling the leggings over, knowing that the teal coloured would suit her. She had stared around the guest room in Anna's apartment, amazed at the cleanliness she hadn't seen in months, the bright cheerful colours of jade and cream. She had inspected the soaker tub and then chosen the large shower, relishing the heat of the water and the selection of shampoos and soaps. The fluffy jade towels had her in tears. She had never known such luxury, she thought.

Doc stood for a moment, his arm around Anna, thankful for his helpmeet, and watched as Berneen slept.

"Any concerns?"

———

Anna shook her head. "No, I don't think so. Physically, I saw a few bruises and her feet are rubbed almost raw in some spots. There are some minor cuts on her hands and feet but they can be dealt with tomorrow. It's her emotional state that I am worried about."

Doc nodded. "I'll look her over tomorrow. Tonight, let her sleep. She may be up and down, but I think we're okay for now." He looked behind him. "Some of the boys will be up, watching over Baird, and will come get us if they need us."

"Good. Head off, Aaron. I'll be along shortly. I just worry about her."

Doc dropped a kiss on his wife's cheek, thinking she was more beautiful than when they had wed in their late teens.

Brady looked up from where he sat near Baird's bed as Doc stopped beside it, his hand reaching for Baird's wrist, and then reaching for his stethoscope.

"Doc?"

Doc looked up at Brady, knowing how close the men on each team were with each other.

"He's hurting, Brady. I won't kid you that way. But he's sleeping naturally. The IV will help rehydrate him." He watched Baird closely before he nodded. "We'll need to keep him quiet for a couple of days. He's had a rough go."

"And the lady?"

"Berneen? Anna finally found out her name. She's hurting emotionally. I'll assess her tomorrow.

We're concerned about her emotional health. You know nothing about her?"

Brady shook his head. "They hadn't seen her. They just couldn't figure out why Baird wouldn't move to the fence. He's the one who wanted her to come, refused to move until they had her with us."

"He'll need to debrief, won't he?" Doc simply shook his head after he spoke and walked away.

Chapter 3

Rolling to his side early the next morning, Baird felt the blankets over him before his hand ran along the sheet, a frown on his face. His eyes opening, he waited for the dizziness to hit him. When it didn't, he rolled to his other side, his eyes on the room, wondering for a moment where he was. He took in the hospital atmosphere and then sat up, abruptly, not knowing if he was still a captive or not. He fumbled for the side rail, finding the lock to release it and lower it before he swung his feet over the edge, looking down to find slippers waiting for him. He stood, slipping into them and then reaching for the robe someone had dropped on the end of the bed, studying it for a moment, thinking it looked familiar before shoving his arms into the sleeves and tightening the belt around his waist.

He shuffled slightly as he walked to the door, not quite steady on his feet, but better than he had been. Cracking open the door, he peeked out and then realized he was home. This was their building. He shot a look behind him and knew he had been taken care of. He just didn't remember much after seeing his team mates drop down in front of him, what day that was, he wasn't sure. He moved towards the stairs, staring at them for a moment before he headed for the elevator, taking it to the third floor, finding his apartment door and entering, sighing as he did so. He spun abruptly, his hand coming out against the wall to

—

21

steady himself as the door opened behind him and Branigan entered.

"Baird? Should you be up?"

Baird stared at him for a moment before he carefully shook his head. "I need to be. I need to get cleaned up." He rubbed at his face, feeling the days-old stubble on it .

Branigan nodded, knowing how he would feel if it had been him. "I can see that, but what has Doc said about you being on your feet?"

Baird went to shake his head again and stopped. "I have no idea. He wasn't there. If you're going to harass me about this, Branigan, leave."

Branigan's hands rose in the air. "No, not that, Baird. Just concern." He nodded down the hallway towards Baird's bedroom. "Go on. Find some clean clothes. Get yourself put back together." He watched carefully as Baird walked away from him, his hand out, tracing along the light cream paint on the hall wall as he walked towards his bedroom, his head hanging down.

Branigan shook his own head. Lord, he shouldn't be on his feet. He's been through something none of the rest of us can understand. He didn't get the care he needed at the first of his trouble. Now, dear Lord, we're playing catch up with that. Help us to help him. He's going to need You like never before, Lord. And I fear this is just beginning for him. Bless my friend, Lord.

He headed for the kitchen, opening first the fridge and then the freezer, finding the cinnamon raisin bagels he knew Baird preferred, finding the toaster tucked away in a cupboard. He listened for the water to stop and then dropped the bagels in the toaster, reaching for the butter and jams to set on the table, making coffee for them both. This kitchen was almost as familiar as his own, the men sharing meals with one another on a frequent basis.

Baird shut the door to his bedroom, leaning on it for a moment, his head back, his eyes closed, knowing just how close to the edge of collapse he was. He didn't remember what he had been through, and wished he did. He needed to process it but couldn't if he didn't know what had happened. He finally moved to his dresser, rifling through the drawers to find clean clothes, staring at a T-shirt for a moment, before he sighed, his eyes closing. He seldom let himself remember his mother but at times when he was down or not well, that was when he wished she was still there, not in heaven. I need her today, Lord. I just need my Mom. He blinked back tears as he headed for the closet, finding clean jeans, and then heading for the attached bathroom, standing for a moment staring at the navy blue towels before he reached to turn on the water in the shower.

Staring at himself in the mirror over the sink a while later, he frowned. He looked haggard, he thought, and then shook his head carefully, waiting for the dizziness to hit once more. He rubbed at his face, knowing he needed to shave but not having the energy to do that. No, he thought, as he tilted his head, he needed to do that, and reached for his razor.

———

Finally heading for the kitchen, following the aroma of the toasted bagels, he paused in the doorway to his spare room, frowning. Something seemed off in there, but he wasn't sure what. He shrugged, heading for the kitchen, a quiet word of thanks for the food.

Branigan eventually pulled him to his feet, a hand on his shoulder directing him back down in the elevator towards the infirmary.

"I don't need to be there, Branigan. I can rest just as well in my own place." Baird's protest echoed through the elevator.

"Doc hasn't released you yet, Baird. You know how it works." He followed Baird from the elevator, watchful as always.

Baird stared down the hallway in one section of the building, where the infirmary was located, noting the door closed to the other infirmary room.

"Branigan? Who got hurt?"

"What do you mean? Who got hurt?" Branigan had a frown on his face, not quite sure what Baird was meaning.

Baird pointed to the door. "There. There's someone in there, isn't there? Which one of our guys got it?"

Branigan's eyes slid shut. Baird had forgotten. Lord, why me? Why do I get to tell him about Berneen? He felt the poke on his shoulder from Baird's finger.

"Branigan?" When his friend didn't respond, Baird turned to the door, tapping quietly. When there was no response, he slowly opened the door, staring inside for a moment before he entered, fully expecting to see one of his team mates there. He could hear water running slowly in the sink in the attached washroom, the door to it open, but his focus was on the bed. His feet carried him forward, slowly, until he stopped, mesmerized by the young woman lying there, asleep. He turned back to stare at the door, Branigan standing in the doorway, his eyes watchful, hands shoved into his sweatshirt pockets.

Baird turned back to the bed, his hands in his cardigan pockets, staring down at the sleeping lady, he guessed to be somewhat his own age. He glanced up briefly to see Anna standing across from him, her eyes on first him and then the lady before she moved away, her feet taking her to Branigan. He could hear their soft conversation, but watched the lady instead.

Who is she, Lord? I know I've seen her but not just sure where. He reached out tentative hands and tucked the blankets up tighter around her neck, seeing her tiny movement away from him and then she lay still, a soft sigh coming from her. He touched a wayward curl that had escaped her braid, marvelling at the softness of her raven black hair, before his hand rested lightly on the side of her face. She shifted slightly, first turning away from his touch, and then leaning into it. He watched carefully, seeing her relax slightly at his touch. And then he saw it. A tear, glistening on her cheek, quivering with the movement of her breathing, reflecting back the light as it moved, momentarily showing a rainbow in its movement. His thumb came out, wiping it gently away, his heart raised

—

in prayer for the lady he didn't know. He turned at last, reluctant to leave her side, but knowing he needed to.

Branigan's hand rested briefly on Baird's shoulder as Baird paused in the doorway to look back at Berneen.

"Branigan?"

"Come on, Baird. You need to get back to bed. You're getting shaky on your feet." Branigan's hand turned his friend towards the other infirmary room. "And I will explain the lady to you."

Baird settled back into the bed, the head of it raised for him to almost sit up. Branigan pulled up a chair, taking a quick look at his watch, knowing he needed to be off to his work shortly, but Baird came first. When he looked up again, Baird had dozed off. Branigan just shook his head and then left, the door closing quietly behind him.

Chapter 4

Mid morning, Bradon Cahill watched Berneen as she stood in the lobby, a look of awe on her face as she slowly turned in a circle, her head raising and lowering as she took in the rich wooden paneling on the walls, the heavy dark green drapes at the windows, carefully selected paintings and framed photographs on the walls, the dark wooden floors, the security counter set off to one side near the corridor that led to the offices. He also knew she would see the seating areas at each end of the lobby, gas fireplaces facing each other from the side walls. He waited for her to turn towards him, leaning a shoulder against the wall near the elevators.

Berneen stopped her circle for a moment, her eyes on a painting and she walked over to take another look. Her eyes slid closed. It was one of her mother's. Tears pushed at her eyelids and she blinked hard to push them back in. She refused to cry. She jumped as she heard a voice beside her and then felt a dog's tongue licking at her hand.

She looked down, staring at the Alsatian standing beside her, looking up at her, mouth open and tongue reaching to lick her hand once more. She carefully touched its head and the dog leaned against her. She looked up startled as she heard the voice again.

"Sorry, I didn't mean to startle you. You seem entranced with that painting." Bradon watched for a moment before he spoke again. "I'm Bradon Cahill.

This dog that seems to have fallen in love with you is my dog, Kade."

"He's beautiful." She looked back at the painting, sorrow coursing through her, causing a frown on Bradon's face. "The painting? I thought it was lost. My mom painted it when I was young. She never told me she had sold it. It just disappeared when I was 18 after they were killed in a riot while overseas."

Bradon stared at her, his eyes finally looking behind her at Barnabas, who stood, shock briefly showing on his face. "Your mother painted this? Barnabas? Berneen, Barnabas Carey is behind you. He's run the foundation here."

Berneen spun, her hands on her face, as she faced Barnabas. "I'm sorry. I'm sorry. I didn't mean to say you stole it. I'm sorry."

The two men stared her, watching carefully as she tried to compose herself.

Barnabas spoke finally, his hand out to take her arm gently. "How be we find seats in my office?"

She stepped back, her head shaking. "No. I can't take your time. Just let me know where I can find a ride to the nearest town and I'll leave."

Barnabas shook his head, as he once more gently took her arm, guiding her down the hallway to his office and seating her in a comfortable chair away from his desk. Bradon sat near her, Kade on the alert, his eyes not leaving Berneen. Barnabas walked away, returning in a short time with a tray of coffee, tea, and cold drinks. He pointed to the tray he set on the table.

"Take your pick." He finally seated himself across the table from her, looking up as he heard a soft tap and then the door opened, Baird appearing, a frown on his face that smoothed out as he saw Berneen. He seated himself near her, realizing as he did so she had not heard him enter, her gaze on Barnabas.

Barnabas watched, a slight smile on his face as Berneen continued to stare at him. "Please, Miss Dakin. Take your pick of what you want. We can't until you do."

She reached for a bottle of water, stopping to stare at the hand that came to rest on her arm.

"Don't take what is closest or easiest. Take what you really want. If it's not there, tell us." Baird's voice startled her and she looked up at him, a frown in place that disappeared, leaving her face blank, as she recognized him.

"You're here?"

"I am." He gave a quick grin before he nodded at the tray. "Now, what do you really want? If it's not there, we'll see if we can find it."

She sighed, not liking that he was forcing her to make a choice. "Is there peppermint tea?"

Baird took a look and then handed her a mug of water and a teabag. "Here. Barnabas always keeps a selection of different teas for whoever wants them. Not all of us like regular tea or coffee."

Berneen took the mug, a quick word of thanks to him, before she looked up at Barnabas, to finding him watching her closely.

—

"Miss Dakin? May I call you Berneen instead?" At her nod, Barnabas grinned. "You'll find we're not much on formalities here." He paused for a moment, his eyes thoughtful. "We need to have a talk, but I think first we need to spend time in prayer."

The men's heads bowed even as Berneen stared at first one and then the other, her eyes finally resting on Baird, sitting close to her, his hand once more on her forearm. She heard a whisper of sound and looked to her other side, to find Kade sitting tight to her, his chin on her leg. She sighed to herself. What now, Lord? What kind of group did I walk into? I'm afraid, Lord, but the fear is not from these men. The fear is from outside. I just know if I leave I'll disappear again and never return.

Chapter 5

Berneen heard the quiet conversation among the three men as she sat, head bowed, her eyes on her mug sitting on the table in front of her, but her thoughts miles away. She jumped slightly as she felt Baird's hand on her arm again and realized then someone had been speaking with her.

"Berneen, Barnabas had asked you a question." Concerned that she didn't respond, he reached to tuck her hair behind her ear, just so he could see her face. "Are you okay?"

Hesitating, she finally shook her head, blinking hard. She refused to cry. Her captivity had taught her that. Any sign of a tear was a reason for belittling, if not a beating, and she just couldn't go through that ever again.

"Berneen, what can we do for you?" Baird shot a look at Barnabas, who had leaned forward in his chair, elbows on his knees, chin on his linked hands. When she didn't respond and wouldn't look at him, he was on his knees beside her, his arm around her, the other hand gently gripping the hands she had clasped on her knee. "What is it you are afraid of? Or who? Or for whom?" He could feel her body shaking, but frowned as he saw her fight with her tears.

"Berneen?" Barnabas' quiet voice had her finally looking up, the men drawing in quick breaths at the look of fear and devastation on her face. "Talk to us. We want to help you. We won't let you fight this on your own. Not anymore. Tell us who you are so scared for."

She shook her head, not wanting to speak, turning her head to watch Baird as Barnabas spoke. He shouldn't be here, she thought, taking in the whiteness of his face, the dark circles under his eyes, the fatigue in his movements.

"Baird, you shouldn't be here."

"No, I need to be. We need to determine who and why. You were just not taken. I get that. It had to be planned. And I was taken for a reason, and I would very much like to know why."

She stared at him. "Sit in your chair, please? You're going to fall over if you don't."

He watched her for a moment before he rose, pulled his chair over as close to her as he could, and then seated himself, reaching for a mug of coffee. He shared a look with Barnabas and Bradon before studying her once more.

"Berneen?" The slight tremor of her hand as she reached for her own mug showed him she had heard him. "What are you afraid of?"

She once more shook her head. "I can't tell you."

"No. It's more than that. You can but you won't." Barnabas smothered a sigh. He was not used to working with women, other than Anna, and his own secretary, Amy. "Who are you afraid for?"

Berneen, in a sudden movement, dropped her mug to the table and was on her feet and out the door, running through the hallways, slamming open the outside door, her feet slipping a bit on the wet step before she was running from the building, not caring or knowing exactly where she was heading.

The three men stood in shock for a moment, and then Baird was right behind her, stopping as he reached the outside, not knowing which way she had run.

"Baird?"

Baird spun as he hear his name called. Blair Campion, a good friend as well as one of the six men on his team, ran towards him, stuffing a rag into his pocket.

"Berneen?" Baird was afraid, afraid that she would disappear before he found her again.

"Towards the lake. I don't know if she even knows where she's heading."

Baird shook his head. "She doesn't. She's terrified for someone and won't tell us." He reached for the jacket Bradon held out, a word of thanks coming from deep within him.

"We'll spread out and find her, Baird. We won't let your lady disappear." Bradon was gone, Kade at his side, leaving Baird staring after him, finally remembering to snap his mouth closed.

"Come on, Baird. I'm with you. The other fellows who are around will be out shortly." Buckley Cullen, the minister in their group who served the community in an old-fashioned stone and clapboard church, stood beside him. "Where to?"

"The lake. I just pray she's safe."

"We all do." Buckley shrugged into his own jacket before pointing to Baird's. "Jacket on, Baird, and then let's move."

"Wait. I need a jacket for Berneen." Baird turned to head back to get one, stopping short as he saw one in Buckley's hands. "Buckley?"

"Anna saw her run and knew she needed this. She handed it to me, told me to stick with you, and to find that child, as she termed it, quickly and bring her home."

Baird nodded, his feet moving him quickly towards the lake. "It will be cold coming in off Lake Erie. I have no idea if she's used to this kind of weather or not."

"She's never said?"

Baird shook his head at the question in Buckley's voice. "We, none of us, have really had a chance to talk to her, it's only been a couple of days. That's what we were doing when she ran. She's afraid for someone and when Barnabas pushed her to tell us, she took off. She's hiding something really deep."

"We all are, Baird, when you come down to it." Buckley slowed his walk, his hand coming out to stop Baird. "Has she family?"

"That we don't know, at least I don't. I imagine by now that Barnabas may have someone looking into that."

—

Chapter 6

Berneen slid to a stop in the sand, her balance off for a moment, as she stared out at the lake. She spun, stumbling slightly in the sand, before she dropped to her knees, not caring that the sand was cold and damp. She rose suddenly, hearing a voice behind her before arms were wrapped tight around her, trapping her own to her body before she was dragged towards a pile of rocks. She struggled to get free but the arms were too strong. A hand was clapped across her mouth to stifle her screams for help. She continued to struggle even as she heard voices.

No, Baird, she thought. Go away. It's too dangerous for you here. She watched, helplessly, as men moved away from the rocks, circling behind Baird and the man with him. She didn't know him, but realized he was a friend of Baird's, trapped now because of her.

"She was here, Buckley. Those are her tracks." Baird searched the area, moving slowly forward, until he saw the disturbance in the sand. "She's been taken again. Where?" His eyes raised as he searched the area, seeing the tracks leading towards the pile of rocks. "Come on. This way."

When Buckley didn't respond, Baird turned to face him, his hands raising into the air as he saw the weapon pointing at Buckley's head and the one pointing at his own.

"Whoa! What's going on here?" Baird frowned when the men didn't respond, merely motioned for him to move. "I'm not moving until you tell me what you want."

He watched as Buckley looked behind him and turned, his hands dropping slightly as he saw Berneen held captive, horror on her face that he had been taken again.

"Again, I have to ask. What is going on?"

Baird received no answer, other than a shove from behind that sent him stumbling through the sand towards Berneen. He could hear mumbling from Buckley behind him. The three were then forced to walk along the beach, almost into the icy waters at times, until they reached a ramshackle cottage and were shoved into it.

Baird was kept separated from the other two, forced to stand near the door, watching closely as Berneen and Buckley stood in the kitchen area, her eyes on him, Buckley watching the men closely. He heard the faint murmurs of talk before he was once more shoved forward, this time back out the door, and then into a waiting vehicle. His heart sank as he twisted to stare back at the cabin, not knowing what was happening and not knowing if he would see those two again.

Left on their own in the cabin, Buckley and Berneen stared at each other for a moment before Buckley made a systematic search of the cabin, turning to face Berneen.

"We haven't been introduced. I'm Buckley and you are Berneen." He grinned at her for a moment. "What happened?"

"What happened? I was grabbed out there, forced to watch you two taken captive, and now I'm left locked up in a cabin. What do you want to know, besides that?" Her words had a bite to them, she was that angry. She sighed. "I apologize. It's not your fault."

"No, it's not. And I don't know that it's either yours or Baird's." Buckley spun to face the door, not sure where Baird had disappeared to. "I suggest we make ourselves as comfortable as we can."

Berneen shrugged, then searched the cabin herself. "There's not much here. No chairs. No couch. Just this table."

"But there is some straw." Buckley scraped it into two piles, and then motioned to her. "Have a seat, my lady. It's rough but it's not the bare floor."

She sank down, grateful for somewhere to sit, her back resting against the rough boards behind her, her arms wrapping around her bent knees. "Why did you follow me?"

Buckley shrugged, a grin appearing on his face for a moment. "Baird was intent on finding you. We couldn't let him go on his own."

She looked at him horrified. "You mean there are more of you out there?"

He nodded. "About six or seven of us. The rest were off site." He tilted his head, a puzzled look on his face. "Why?"

She just shook her head. "You can't be doing that. You just can't."

"And why not? It's who we are, Berneen. We don't walk away from anyone."

"Well, you should. I've brought danger to Baird, I think."

He watched her closely, a frown on his face. "Why would you say that? Maybe it's the other way around. Baird brought danger to you."

She stared at him, remembering to snap her mouth closed. "In case you forgot, I was there when they brought Baird in. So it has to be me."

Buckley shook his head, his heart raising in prayer for Berneen. "Maybe. Maybe not." He looked towards the door as he heard voices and the door swung open, Baird shoved through it, stumbling a bit as he struggled to keep his balance. Buckley was on his feet, fists clenched, ready to fight for his friend, pausing as he saw the weapon pointing at Berneen.

Baird shook his head at Buckley, reaching to wipe at the blood dripping from a cut on his cheek, a bleak look on his face. It had not gone easy with him, not when he realized what they were asking of him. His refusal had gone hard with him. With the escalating threats against Berneen, he had just finally nodded, not willing to put her in any more danger than she was.

Berneen stood as well, tight to the wall, her hands covering her mouth, eyes huge and full of fear and worry, as she stared first at Baird ,then at the man behind him.

"You'll do what we ask, Miss Dakin, or he dies." The voice was low, harsh, and full of menace. The eyes showing through the mask were hard, cold, reminding her of the ice that would soon envelope the lake.

"I don't know what you mean." She gave a small scream as a heavy fist drove itself into Baird's abdomen, bending him forward at the waist. "What did you do that for?" Anger laced her words.

Chapter 7

Berneen kept shaking her head at the escalating demands made towards her, struggling to release herself from the strong arm around her, her eyes flickering towards Buckley, who stood, weapon to his chest, unable to help either one, his mind racing to find a solution and finding none, and then to Baird, who took a blow somewhere on his body each time she refused a request.

The final blow Baird took sent him to his knees, bent over at the waist, sitting back on his legs even as his arms wrapped around his abdomen, his head touching the dirty, worn wood floor. Blood dripped from the cuts on his face and from his lip, bruising beginning to show.

Berneen grasped the thumb of the man holding her, pulling it backwards as far and as hard as she could. A cry of pain sounded from the man and his arm loosened enough so that she could shove away from him and scurry to Baird. She dropped to her knees, her arms around Baird, her head buried against his neck as sobs shook her body. Buckley moved to try and get to them but stopped as he felt the weapon dig harder into his chest. His heart broke for Berneen as he listened to her sob-filled pleas for Baird not to be hurt anymore, for them not to kill him.

"It's your choice, Miss Dakin. You do what we want, he lives. You refuse once more and he dies." The man who spoke studied his nails, not really caring which way she decided. He had been given his orders and he was following them.

Berneen finally nodded, agreeing to their demands. She was pulled to her feet, her hands reaching for Baird as he too was hauled upright, her arms around him to help steady him as he swayed.

Buckley made a sound, drawing her attention to him, shaking his head at her. "Berneen. No."

"I have to, Buckley. There's no other way." She caught her breath, trying to still the sobs. "He'll die if I don't."

"That is correct, Miss Dakin. Your decision has saved his life, for now."

She stared at the man, unable to see his face for the mask he wore, shudders running through him. "I don't understand."

"You will." He turned to one of his men, who held out a paper for him. "We have the license. We have the minister. Let's have a wedding."

Berneen turned to Baird, sobs shaking her body once more. "Baird?"

"It's okay, Neen. We're okay." His voice was low, halting, and he had difficulty forming his words.

Buckley was shoved towards them, barely keeping his balance. He studied his friend and then Berneen, sighing to himself, knowing there was no way out of this. Not unless someone friendly walked through the door right now and he couldn't count on that. His heart raised in prayer, asking for guidance, for permission to perform the ceremony, but knowing he had little choice.

"Buckley?" Berneen's broken question caught his attention. "Who's the minister?"

"That would be him." The leader of the men shoved at Buckley, causing him to sway slightly. "He's a minister. Much better than a JP."

Berneen stared at Buckley, horror on her face for a moment. "You're a minister? Is that why they took you?"

He shook his head. "No, I just happened to be there." He sighed, rubbing his hands up and down his arms. "Are you sure, Berneen? Baird?"

Baird mumbled something, his consciousness fading a bit more with each moment. Buckley sighed once more. It was now or never, he thought. *Lord, I have no idea what Your plans are for my friend and this young lady. Please, Lord? Is there any way to avoid this?*

Buckley stood for a moment, his eyes closed, before he felt the weapon poke him once more in the back. He sighed, his eyes opening, taking in his friend and the young woman standing beside him, knowing he had no choice but to perform the ceremony.

The words spoken, the "I do's" said, signatures on the paper, Buckley finally drew a deep breath. He had no idea what to expect at this point. A sudden sound from Berneen had him reaching for Baird, catching at him as he fell forward, taking Berneen with him. The couple hit the floor with a thud and lay still,

—

Buckley prevented from reaching them. He was shoved backwards into the wall, his own vision darkening and swirling in front of him as his head hit a stud and then he too was still, his eyes open but his body not responding to his commands. He didn't feel the paper tucked into his jacket nor hear the men leave.

Buckley finally roused, shivering in the chilliness of the cabin. He scrubbed at his face, as his eyes searched for the men and not seeing them. He was on his feet, stumbling towards Baird and Berneen, dropping to his knees to feel for pulses. His head dropped to his chest as he realized they were still alive.

Berneen roused slightly, her head raising before it dropped once more to her out-flung arm. Buckley sat back on his heels, his eyes assessing the two, before he rose and headed for the door, not knowing if the captors were out there or not. A sound at the door stopped his progress in mid-step and he raised his hands, fisted, in an effort to be ready to protect himself. His hands dropped as he recognized the men coming through the doorway.

"Brady! Bradon! Brody! Burney! What? How did you find us?"

Brady shook his head as he took a swift look at Buckley. "You okay?"

"I am, I guess. It's Baird. He took an awful beating."

Brady was on his knees beside Baird, assessing him, before he turned to Berneen. "How long, Buckley?"

"I'm not sure. A couple of hours at least. What day is it?"

"It's Tuesday." Bradon Cahill watched Buckley closely.

"Late Tuesday?"

Bradon shook his head. "No, early morning. The sun's just up."

"Then twelve hours, maybe?" He started for the door, Brody Corcoran after him. "Where are they?"

"Who, Buckley?"

"The five men. They were here. Where are they?"

"Gone. What happened?" Burney Cummins was torn, not sure whether to follow his team mates or wait with Brady.

Buckley shook his head. "First, those two need seen to. Brady? Can we just take them to Doc?" He was desperate to get out of there but didn't know if Baird could or should even be moved.

"We can, for now, Buckley." Brady stood, his eyes on the couple. "Let's get them out of here. Brody, Burney. You two take Baird. I'll take Berneen."

Buckley followed them, not sure of anything anymore, other than they needed to be out of there.

Berneen roused as she was buckled into a seat, fighting against the hands holding her. "I need to stay with Baird. Please? Where's Baird? I can't leave him."

Brady sat back on his heels, before he turned to look at Buckley. "Buckley? What is she talking about?"

Buckley just shook his head. "I need to talk to Barnabas." His head dropped back against the headrest and his eyes closed.

Chapter 8

Barnabas stood, his eyes on Buckley, not quite sure he understood what the other man had said, fingering the folded paper he had been handed. Buckley leaned against the wall outside the infirmary room, his head back, his eyes closed, fatigue in every line of his posture.

Looking through the open door, Barnabas watched as Doc and Brady worked over Baird. He could tell their concern by their movements, even though he couldn't hear their words. His eyes lifted to where Berneen stood at the head of the bed, not moving, her eyes on Baird, her hands clenched around the railing of the bed. She swayed too with fatigue and something else Barnabas couldn't put his finger on. She had been adamant when they tried to separate the couple. She just refused. When they had physically removed her, she fought them, finding her freedom from them and running back into the room, to stand where he now saw her. Doc had looked at him and just shook his head, stating that they should just let her be for now.

"What are you saying, Buckley?" Barnabas' attention went back to his friend.

"They're married, Barnabas. They forced me to marry them. They almost killed Baird before she agreed." Buckley looked up, devastation in his eyes as well as worry and something else Barnabas just couldn't place, shame, perhaps? "I had no choice." He

———

nodded to the paper. "They took Baird away first and then came back with that."

"Married?" Barnabas unfolded the paper, reading it, before he folded it again and dropped it into a pocket on his shirt. "It's legal?"

Buckley nodded. "They made sure of that. I suspect when they took Baird away, that's what they went and did. I don't remember Berneen signing anything though."

"This sounds as if it was well planned. She could have signed the application when she was held captive the first time, without knowing what it was she was signing. This sounds like a sophisticated group."

Buckley shook his head, even as he shoved himself away from the wall. "I'm not seeing that. I see revenge in it." He walked away, shoulders stooped with fatigue and another emotion he refused to admit to.

Barnabas watched him go, seeing Breck walking up beside Buckley, before he turned and walked towards the bed where Baird lay.

"Doc?"

Doc looked up for a moment, then swinging his stethoscope around his neck, he walked to where Barnabas stood at the end of the bed.

"He's hurt, Barnabas. He'll heal but it will take a while. No broken bones. I don't see any evidence of internal bleeding. Whoever did this was a pro."

"That's what I was thinking. Has he spoken at all?"

—

Doc nodded. "Just to ask where Berneen was. When he found out she was safe and standing near him, he just nodded and passed out again." He paused, not quite sure how to express himself. "Barnabas, what do you know of what happened? They're both wearing rings, wedding bands, that they weren't yesterday morning."

Barnabas drew a deep breath, knowing his next words would be a shock, and would change the dynamics of their group. "Buckley married them. He was forced to. From what he said, if Berneen had not agreed, we would be having a funeral for Baird."

Doc stared at him for a moment, no longer shocked by what he heard anymore, working as he did in a low-cost clinic in the downtown area of their nearby town. "You're sure?"

"We are. Buckley said if he hadn't agreed, they would have found some other way to make it happen. He gave me the license. I'll check it out but I would suspect the marriage is already registered. They're not amateurs, whoever they are."

Brady had moved closer to them, a frown on his face. "But why? Why Baird? Why Berneen?"

"That's what we'll need to investigate, Brady. Some of the guys are already at work on that, without knowing the full extent of what the three went through. We'll meeting in ten minutes in the boardroom."

"I'll be there." Brady walked away, his head shaking at the news.

"What about Berneen, Doc?" Barnabas studied her, moving quickly to catch her as she swayed and then collapsed. He looked around for somewhere to set her, moving to the recliner Doc pushed towards the bed.

"She won't move from the room, Barnabas. And I would like to know why."

"Buckley said she was threatened after he finished the ceremony. She was told she had to stay with Baird at all times. If she didn't, he would be dead. Just like that."

"What?" Doc stared at him even as he reached to assess Berneen. "Who does this? This young lady has been through enough already."

"I know. But she's still hiding something. She's afraid for someone and won't tell us who."

"She's an orphan, right?" When Barnabas nodded, Doc continued. "I don't see a boy friend, so it must be a sibling. Have you looked into that?"

"We are now. I spoke with the police. They're not saying much, but they don't have much to go on. No one reported her missing and we think she was held for at least three months, just for what little she has said."

"A brother." Baird's soft voice interrupted them.

"What was that, Baird?" Barnabas walked to the head of the bed, bending over to catch Baird's words.

"A brother. Darby. She whispered his name when we were in the cabin. I don't know where he is though."

"We'll find him." Barnabas straightened up, his eyes on Berneen. "We'll find him and bring him to her, to safety." He spun on his heel and walked rapidly from the room, knowing that he needed to speak with the other twelve men and send them searching for Darby.

Chapter 9

Pausing in the doorway to the conference room, Barnabas drew a deep breath. He watched the eleven men who were working away, laptops, phones, tablets in front of them. He could see someone had been using the whiteboards as well. He gave a small smile as he watched Burney Cummins working away with pen and paper. As an author, Burney thought differently from the other men and worked with what he called old-school tools. Breck stood beside him, concern on his face. Barnabas knew that when he spoke, what he would have to change would change the dynamics of the group. This was not how he ever thought it would, but God knew, he understood. God had allowed this, why, he had no idea.

Breck finally spoke. "Barnabas?"

"Yeah, Breck?"

"What happened out there? Buckley won't say, Baird isn't talking, and Berneen won't leave his side. She fought us too hard to get back to him for it to be something minor."

—

"It's something major, Breck." He sighed, raising a quick prayer for words and guidance before he walked over to drop into the chair at the head of the table, his eyes searching each man's face as they looked up at him.

"Guys. We need to talk. But first we need to pray and pray hard. What I have to tell you is not easy."

An hour later, Barnabas rose, heading for the table that held the coffee pot and the kettle. He hesitated for a moment, his head dropping down as he thought through what had happened in a week or so. He sighed to himself before he picked up his mug and turned watching as the men milled around, each uncertain as to what was coming. He finally dropped back into his seat, watching closely as the men selected their tea or coffee of choice and then sat back down, their eyes on him. Breck had left for a moment and was even now heading back into the room, a sheaf of papers in his hand that he set down in front of Barnabas.

Barnabas drew a deep breath, one of the deepest he thought he had ever had to draw.

"Guys. This is not easy. Our group dynamics have changed, without our input. Yesterday, while Baird, Buckley and Berneen were held captive, Baird was beaten severely. You all know that. What you don't know is why. And this is so hard. It affects Baird in a way I never thought it would. Berneen was asked a question and every time she refused, Baird was beaten. She finally agreed to their demands. What were their demands? That she marry Baird." He waited as he heard the indrawn breaths, the quiet comments, and the questions that spilled from the men. He finally held up a hand. "Buckley told me she had no choice. If she hadn't finally agreed, Baird would not be here. They were adamant that she do what they demanded, or Baird would be killed. Buckley was forced to perform the ceremony, even though he resisted. We have no idea as to why or who yet. That's what we need to dig in and find out."

He nodded as Benen Carroll raised a hand. "What do we know about Berneen? Other than what we have been told by her, and that's not a lot."

Barnabas shook his head. "We're finding out more. She was afraid for someone, we can all agree on that. It is her brother, Darby. Baird was awake enough to tell me that. Where he is, that we need to find."

"Do we know how old he is? What he looks like?" Branigan was reaching for his laptop, already to search.

"We don't know that. That's what we need to find out. We do know that she is an orphan, she's admitted to that."

"How long?" This from Blair, who was reaching for his phone, searching for newspaper articles.

"I'm not sure, but I would suspect a while." Breck finally spoke. "If he's younger than her, she would have likely had custody of him."

Brody spoke up, looking up from his phone. "She was 18 when her parents died. Apparently it was in a riot overseas." He drew in a deep breath, looking up at Barnabas, sorrow and worry combined on his face. "Her brother was only five."

"Five?" Barnabas too drew in a deep breath before he shoved back from the table. "Find out everything you can and get it to me as soon as you can. I'm heading to see if Berneen is awake."

Barnabas hesitated in the doorway of the infirmary room, not sure how to proceed. He walked forward, stopping by Baird's side, watching as he moved restlessly in his sleep. He walked around the bed and crouched down in front of Berneen, finding her awake.

"Berneen?" He watched as her eyes moved to him and a look of devastation and shame came across her face. "We don't blame you. Not one of us. We thank you for keeping Baird alive. Buckley told us what happened." He watched as her eyes slid closed, her throat working as she swallowed hard, tears trickling down her face. He reached out for a damp cloth that sat on a table beside her and handed it to her, watching as she twisted it in her hands.

"I'm so sorry, Barnabas. I can't imagine what the other men think." She looked up at him, tears clouding her eyes. "I tried to stop them. I didn't want to do this. They would have killed him. I couldn't let them do that."

"We know that, Berneen. None of us blame you. We want to help you." He watched her closely.

She looked over at the bed. "How is Baird?"

"He's alive. He's hurting but he will for a while. Now, Berneen, we need to talk. Baird mentioned your brother's name. You said it when you were trying to protect him."

"I was. Someone threatened us. I had to hide him."

"Do you know who?"

She hesitated, then shrugged. "I'm not sure. I think the lawyer was involved." She turned as she heard a sound and then was on her feet, bending over Baird as he roused. "Baird?"

"Neen? Are you okay?" His words were barely audible and he slipped into a natural sleep before she could answer.

"Baird? Baird?" Berneen made a sound of disappointment before she felt Barnabas' arm around her shoulders.

"Berneen, can you come with us? I know. I know. You were told not to leave his side, but I have security at his door. No one will get to him. We need to talk to you and I want the other men to hear what you have to say."

She stared at him in horror. "Oh, no! I can't face them. Look what I did!"

Breck spoke from beside her. "You did nothing wrong. Not that we are aware of. The other guys know that. They all want to see you, to speak with you."

Barnabas' arm around her shoulders drew her away, much to her distress, and then he guided her to the conference room where the men were working away. He noted with no surprise that Buckley was there, providing the encouragement they all needed. He made a mental note to talk to Buckley himself or have his father do that.

Chapter 10

Barnabas seated Berneen at the table, setting a cup of the peppermint tea she seemed to prefer in front of her before he stepped away to speak with Breck. She refused to raise her eyes, not wanting to see the looks of condemnation she was sure she would see.

"Berneen?" Buckley's low voice caught her attention. "Are you okay?"

"I think so. I'm not sure."

Barnabas slid into the chair beside her, his eyes on her, knowing the men were watching her.

"Berneen, can you look up for a moment?" When she didn't respond, he repeated himself. "Baird would want you to."

She hesitated, then finally raised her head, dreading the looks she just knew she would be facing. She sought the faces of each man, reading in each one their compassion for her and their concern. She shook her head. "I shouldn't be here."

"No, you need to be." Barnabas sipped at his mug of coffee before he set it back down. "First, before we do anything else, Buckley?"

Buckley nodded, his head bowing as he petitioned God for peace for the young woman seated at the table and for each one of them, for wisdom as they sought answers, for protection for them all.

———

Barnabas hesitated for a moment before he began to speak.

"I need to explain our situation here. It's a unique group of men I have working for me."

Berneen's eyes were trained on him, a puzzled look on her face.

"The Barnabas Foundation was started by my father when I was born, named for me, but based on the Barnabas in the Bible. It was set up to encourage people to get ahead. He provided no-cost loans and grants to organizations, churches, individuals, etc, who needed them. When he retired and I took over the Foundation, we changed how it works. I employ these men. They work in various occupations in the community but their wages come from the Foundation. They are also volunteers in various groups in the community, being mentors, those who come along side of those who need their help and encouragement. We take no credit for what we do. That credit belongs to God. We meet weekly for a time of prayer to refresh ourselves and then to search through the applications and requests that we receive for help."

"Just men?" Berneen's quiet question had Barnabas pausing, his eyes on her.

"That's correct. It is hoped that as the men meet their life mates and marry, we can expand our services to women and children. That is what our prayer is." Barnabas watched as her eyes slid closed and she reached to swipe at the tears on her face. "Berneen?"

"I wish you had been doing that for women and children. I could have used your help." Her head went down on her folded arms when she finished speaking.

"Berneen? Can you tell us your story? We all want to help you. You're part of our family now."

She looked up at Breck as he spoke, her head shaking. "No, I'm not. I'm an interloper."

Breck shook his head, a slight smile on his face. "No, you're family. Talk to us, please? The men have been searching, finding bits and pieces, but there are things that you know that we won't find, no matter how we search."

She watched Breck as he spoke, knowing he was speaking from his heart and that she really did need to talk to them. She sighed, not seeing the looks the men were exchanging, puzzled looks to be true, but with compassion on their faces. She finally nodded, and when she spoke, her voice was low and broken.

"I have to go back a few years. Mom and Dad were wonderful. Dad provided well for us, and always had everything in order. That's why what happened after they died puzzled me so much.

"Dad had to go overseas on business. For some reason, he really didn't want to go, but went. Mom went with him. While there a riot broke out. They were killed. But they were the only ones hurt or killed." She looked up at Barnabas. "That was just so strange. Their bodies were brought home. The day after the funeral, the lawyer approached me, told me the house and everything in it was gone and we had to leave right away. He gave me thirty minutes to pack what I could and what I needed for Darby before he shoved us into his car and then dropped us off downtown, with nowhere to go and nowhere to stay." She blinked back tears as she stared up at the ceiling. "How do you explain to someone that their parents are gone and now their home is?"

"Berneen, how old were you?"

'Eighteen." She looked at Barnabas as she answered his question, not hearing the quickly indrawn breaths from the men.

"And Darby?"

She shook her head, tears making it impossible for her to speak for a moment. "Five. Dad had changed things so I became his guardian if anything happened to them."

"Eighteen and suddenly responsible for a child. Did you have a boyfriend?" Breck's quiet question startled the other men for a moment.

She nodded. "I did. Until he found out I wouldn't put Darby into foster care. He pushed for that. When I refused, told him he was my only lying relative left, that I wouldn't let him go, he laughed at me and walked away. Told me that no man wanted to be saddled with a child."

She once more didn't see the thunderous looks of anger on the men's faces as they shared glances, or hear the angry mutterings. Barnabas did, but watched Berneen closely.

"How did you survive?" Breck asked the question the other men wanted to but didn't ask.

"For the first couple of nights we slept in abandoned buildings. Then I was able to get into a shelter. I had to prove over and over that I had custody of Darby. Finally, someone helped me to find a furnished room and work at a convenience store. It was a struggle, still is. I wanted to go to college, but won't, not while I have to provide for Darby."

"And where is Darby now?" Barnabas waited for an answer, seeing her struggling with whether to trust him or not. "Berneen? Where is Darby?"

"So far, I think he's safe, but it's been three months since I saw him, so I don't know for sure." She raised her eyes to Barnabas. "I need to see him, to see he's okay."

"We'll find him and bring him to you. Trust us, he'll come to no harm. Just tell us where he is."

Berneen studied his face before she raised her eyes and did the same to each man seated there, finally realizing that for now she was safe and that Darby would be to.

She sighed, reaching for a paper, writing down an address. "There is one thing. He won't come willingly unless you give him the code words."

"Code words? Not just one?" This comment came from Brandon Conaghan.

She nodded. "It's what he wanted. He wanted to be safe and he felt if we had a system of words then no one could persuade him to go with them." She reached for a pad of paper and dashed off a quick note. "Give him this, after you give the code words."

———

61

Barnabas nodded to the men he wanted to go. Brandon stopped by Berneen.

"What are the words, Berneen?" His words were quiet as he reached for the folded paper.

"They are carnation and daisy." She sighed, a slight smile on her face. "He wanted flowers and would only take the names of the ones I like best. There is a phrase as well." She paused, sorrow flicking across her face. "It's like this: Go with Berneen. Mom and Dad. He chose it as well." She rose suddenly and ran from the room, seeking solace with Baird.

Chapter 11

Her head resting against the pillow, Berneen pulled the blanket up over her more, her eyes on Baird as he tossed and turned, his sleep restless. She wasn't thinking of anything, keeping her mind blank on purpose, not sure if Barnabas would be successful in finding and convincing Darby to go with his men. She looked around at the quiet steps, a frown coming on her face as she saw Breck with one of the other men.

"Berneen? We have a question for you. Buckley said you were told not to leave Baird at all. How do they know if you do?" Breck's question caught at her thoughts and she shrugged.

"I have no idea."

"Do you have any other jewelry other than your rings?"

She finally nodded, her hand reaching for a necklace that she wore. "Just this."

"Can we see it for a moment?" He waited until she nodded and then took it off, handing it to him.

Branigan reached for it, inspecting it before he nodded. "What we thought, Breck. There's something here that would track her. I can remove it." He walked away with her necklace, leaving her staring after him.

"Hey, wait! You can't take that." She shoved at her blanket, her hands stilling as she saw Breck shaking his head. "What? Did he really just do that?"

—

"He did, Berneen. He'll be right back with your necklace. I promise. There's a tag of some kind on it that tracks you."

Her face paled, and she drew in a deep breath. "How long?"

Breck shrugged. "We don't know that. Not until we catch the men responsible." He shot a quick glance back at the door. "Can you give us any names?"

She sighed. "You're not giving up on that, are you?" When he grinned at her and shook his head, she stared at him. "Okay. The lawyer is Owen Small. I don't know of any others."

She didn't see the closed look come over Branigan's face at the name or the look the two men exchanged. That was a name they knew, had been looking into for a long time, just waiting to find something to hold him responsible for what they suspected.

"Have they found Darby?" She looked up at Breck with a plea on her face.

"Not yet. They're searching for him. They haven't gone to the house door yet, not wanting to spook him or let someone know where he is." Breck turned slightly as he heard a sound. "Excuse me."

Berneen rose, moving to stand beside Baird, watching as he awakened slightly, her hand reaching for his. Baird's eyes flicked open, and she could tell he was more aware of where he was.

"Baird?" Her soft voice drew his attention to her.

"Berneen? Where are we?"

"You are in the infirmary at your home. I just happen to be here as well." She watched closely as he nodded before glancing around and then reaching to raise the head of the bed. "How are you feeling?"

"Sore, but I want out of here. Where's Doc?"

"He won't be back until this afternoon." Breck stood at the end of the bed, assessing Baird. "You're not going anywhere until he says you can."

Baird's head went back as he groaned. "I need out of here, Breck. I need to keep Berneen safe. I can't do that from here."

"We hear you, Baird, but no, not until Doc comes back." Breck excused himself as he heard his name called.

"Berneen? Help me up, please?"

"No, you need to be here." Her hand on his stilled his motions. "Let me see if I can find something for you to eat."

He shook his head. "No, don't leave me."

Breck had returned, his face thoughtful, as he approached the bed. "Why is it so important that she not leave you?"

"They told me that if she did, she would die." Baird looked up at the silence that greeted his words. "What?"

"When did they tell you that?"

"When we were separated. Why?"

"Because I was told the very same thing after they made us marry. Who are these monsters?" Berneen ran from the room, not sure where she was heading, but finding her way to the chapel on the main floor of the building. She slid into a seat, her arms wrapped around herself, not sure if she should be there, but not knowing where else to go.

Chapter 12

Brandon watched the young man approaching them, his eyes dropping to a photo he held before he tucked it away in his jacket pocket. He nodded to Benen, Blair and Brady, knowing that Darby Dakin was nearing them. He deliberately stepped into Darby's path, causing the youth to stop suddenly and look up at him, fear flickering briefly in his eyes.

"Excuse me? I need to pass, please." Darby stood, waiting for the men to move, frowning when they didn't. "I'm sorry. I really do need to go by you." He moved to the side, finding his way still blocked. "Is there a problem?"

Brandon finally spoke, a smile playing across his face. "If you're Darby Dakin, and I have no doubt you are, we need to talk." He watched closely Darby's face, seeing a slight quiver on the lips. "Your sister sent us."

Darby remained still, his eyes trained on Brandon, but noting the three other men.

Brandon grinned. "Berneen was right. She said you wouldn't respond. Here are the words she gave us. Carnation. Daisy. And a phrase. Go with Berneen. Mom and Dad." He watched as Darby's shoulders slumped and put out a hand to steady the youth.

"She's safe?" Darby's desperate question was barely above a whisper. "I haven't heard from her in weeks."

"She's safe. Now, do you need to go into the house or can you come with us right away?" Benen spoke from beside Darby.

"No. I carry everything with me. She told me to."

"Prepared. Good. We like that." Been gentle hand shoved him into the car. "In you go. We'll take you to your sister."

"She's okay? She's not hurt?" Darby was anxious, desperate to know how his sister was. She was the only relative he knew. He could barely remember his parents.

"She has had what you might call an adventure." Brandon turned to him, his eyes meeting first Blair who was behind the wheel, taking them away from the house and towards Berneen. "She was kidnapped and held captive. Some of us men managed to get her free."

"Kidnapped? When? Three months ago? That's when she stopped communicating with me."

"That sounds about right." Brady finally spoke, his eyes having assessed Darby's condition as best he could. "Do you know anything about who would want to do that?"

Darby's face darkened. "That lawyer. Or her boyfriend from when we had to leave the house. He was nasty to me. Berneen never saw what he did and I was too scared to say anything."

"He's not in the picture as far as Berneen in concerned." The four men exchanged a glance before

Brady sighed. "We have to tell you something though. Your sister was married yesterday. Not by choice. She chose to do that to save the life of a friend of ours."

"Married?" Darby's voice rose sharply. "How? No way!"

"I'm sorry, Darby." Brandon's soft voice caught his attention. "She is. Baird was beaten almost to death."

"It can't be legal, can it?" Darby's eyes searched each of the men's faces before he slumped back against the seat. "It's not. It can't be."

"I'm sorry, Darby." Brady's voice cut through his dark thoughts. "A friend of ours was forced to perform the ceremony. Whoever the men were who had abducted the three of them made sure it was done legally. We searched. The marriage is recorded as happening."

Darby's face was buried in his hands by the time Brady finished. "This can't be happening. Why Berneen?"

"That's what we're working through to find out. If you know anything, we'll want to talk to you."

Darby was silent, his thoughts in disarray. "I need to see Neen." His voice was barely above a whisper, as he stared through the windshield, watching as the darkness deepened and the stars came out. "I just need Neen."

The men nodded soberly, knowing she needed her brother as well.

Brady led Darby quietly through the hallways of the building, stopping for a moment at the infirmary door. "They should be here. Doc wasn't sure if he would let Baird go to his apartment or not." He cracked open the door and paused. "It looks as if he let them go."

He turned Darby around, walking with him towards the elevator, hesitating as he saw Barnabas heading their way.

"Darby, this is Barnabas. He's the one we work for."

Darby studied the older man before his hand went out for Barnabas to shake. "Thank you. Thank you for finding Berneen. Where is she?"

"Doc released Baird and let him go home. They're upstairs in his apartment. That's where Brady's taking you." Barnabas watched as the youth struggled to control his emotions, not willing to cry in front of the older men. "Come on, Darby. We'll get you to your sister in a couple of minutes."

Barnabas tapped lightly at the apartment door and then opened it, moving through with Darby and Brady following. He paused as he heard heated words from the couple in the living room. He watched their standoff for a moment before he spoke.

"Baird. Berneen. Stop, you two. I have someone here who wants to see Berneen."

The words halted as Baird looked towards the three standing in the entranceway, Berneen not moving.

"Berneen? Sweetheart?" Baird's voice finally broke through her stillness. "I think you need to turn around. Sweetheart? Please?"

She glared at him. "I'm not your sweetheart." She finally turned, not sure what or who was there, her hands flying to her face as she saw Darby and then she was across the floor, sobs shaking her body as the siblings clung to each other, Darby's face wet as well from his tears.

Chapter 13

Berneen tried to control her sobs, bring her emotions back under control, knowing she needed to do that, not just for herself but for her beloved brother. Her thanks raised to God, knowing He was the one who had kept her brother safe and brought him back to her. She looked up at Brady, mouthing her thanks to him. He nodded, spoke quietly to Barnabas and Baird and then walked away, closing the door quietly behind him.

Berneen finally stood back, her arms wrapped around herself as she studied her brother.

"Darby? You're okay?"

He nodded, not wanting to trouble her with the feeling he had been followed more than once.

"No, you're not. How many times?"

"A few. I couldn't see them but I know someone was there." He lifted his eyes to Barnabas. "I was followed. I don't know why."

"That's okay, we'll figure it out. Right now, though, I think you're needing something to eat. Come on. Baird won't mind if we raid his fridge. I hope he has something besides bagels and cream cheese." Barnabas winked at Darby as he turned the younger man towards the kitchen, laughing at Baird's protest that the fridge was stocked, Anna had seen to that.

Baird watched Berneen closely for a moment before he approached and just enveloped her into a hug. She clung to him, her tears wetting his shirt once more.

"You okay?" His voice was low enough so that only she could hear him.

"I'm not sure, Baird. Not anymore. I'm glad Darby's here, but it just complicates things."

His chin on the top of her head, he sighed, tightening his hold on her. "It does, but we'll work it through. Do you want him here with you or do you want him to stay with Doc and Anna?"

"Here. I can't leave him anymore." She gave a groan of frustration. "This is so unfair, Baird."

"I know, Sweetheart. I know. You've been shoved into something you don't want, may never want, and don't know why or who."

She finally stepped back, almost running for the bathroom. He could heard the tap running, knowing she was seeking to control her emotions. He sighed, his gaze looking up as he sought wisdom from God as to what he did or didn't do. He finally moved towards the kitchen, peace in his heart, but hurting physically. He was ready to lay down again, to take some pain medications, but he was reluctant to, not until he had talked to Barnabas.

Barnabas shoved away from the counter he had been leaning against, holding out a mug for Baird. Baird nodded, his eyes on Darby.

"Where am I to go?" Darby's question caught the two men off guard for a moment. "I mean, you just got married, right?"

Baird pulled back the chair beside Darby, and slid down, grateful to be off his feet, his eyes closing for a moment against the pain. Barnabas watched, a frown on his face, as he searched Baird's face, seeing the deepening colours of the bruises, the cuts and scrapes from his beating.

"Berneen wants you to stay here. We'll work it out, Darby. You two need each other." Baird laid a hand on the youth's arm. "You two have healing you need to do. We'll keep you as safe as we can here."

"But I have school. How do I go back and forth?" Darby ignored Baird's words for the moment.

"We'll work out something that you can do here. Baird here mentors young men in high school."

"You do?" Darby was surprised. "As a volunteer?"

"That's correct. We all have normal occupations but we all volunteer in an organization that helps encourage others to get ahead." Baird's eyes slid closed and he swayed slightly in his chair.

Barnabas moved towards Baird, pulling him to his feet, and then directing him down the hall, meeting Berneen as she walked towards them.

"Baird?"

"He needs to be laying down, Berneen. I'll get him settled." Barnabas shot a glance behind him.

"You need to talk to Darby. He's not sure where he should be."

She nodded, her eyes on Baird, her thoughts muddled as to which of the men who she now had in her life that she should go to. She walked towards the kitchen, watching Darby as he moved around, making himself another sandwich, and saw his look of gloom and defeat and worry.

"Darby?"

Darby spun, his eyes on his sister. "Neen?"

"We'll talk, Darb. Tonight, I've made up the guest room for you. Not that I had to do much. Baird is so prepared for anything and everything it seems."

"We do need to talk, Neen. I tried to find you, but couldn't." He blinked rapidly, not willing for the tears to fall again. "I just need to understand what happened to you."

"I'm not sure I even know. Once you're done that sandwich, head off for bed. I left the light on for you."

"Neen?" She turned back at his questioning voice. "Are you okay? I mean, with marrying like you did. The men who found me told me what happened. It shouldn't have been that way."

"I know, Darb. But God allowed it. He could have stepped in at any time. We'll work it through." She turned as Barnabas stopped beside her. "Baird's settled?"

"He is. He almost refused his pain medications but thought better of that idea." Barnabas studied the young woman in front of him, sorrow in his heart for what his friend and his lady had been put through. "We'll talk more tomorrow, Berneen." He walked away, leaving the siblings staring after him.

Chapter 14

Snuggling down further under the blanket, Berneen laid her head against the pillow she had dropped on the living room couch earlier, a yawn drawn from her. She glanced at the clock, only two in the morning, she thought. It's been a long night and it's not over. She had been up and down, making sure her men were asleep.

She had just gotten Baird settled again. He had been up and had refused her requests to take his pain medications until the pain had almost doubled him over. It had taken a while to work but she knew he was sleeping now. He had wanted to talk and she had refused, knowing his body needed the sleep, that he wasn't ready to hear what she had to say. And just what did she have to say, she wondered?

She had stopped to check on Darby on her way back to the living room, dropping to her knees beside his bed, a hand on his hair, desperate pleas raised to God. She knew what she was facing was far from over. That was a given, she thought. She just wanted her men safe. She didn't care about herself.

She reached for her Bible, her hand rubbing along the well-worn leather. She had left it with Darby when she sent him into hiding. She blinked rapidly for a moment, willing the tears away. I've cried enough, she decided. I need to be strong and not cry at anything anymore. Lord, where do I search for help? What verses do I go to? I know You've promised safety, that

I am never alone, but some days it feels like that. I need to have something I can cling to, a verse or verses, something, please, dear Lord.

She lifted her head hours later, then shoving back her blanket, stumbled to her feet, running for Baird as she heard muttering coming from him. Darby met her in the hallway.

"Berneen?"

"It's Baird." She shoved the door to the bedroom all the way open and was on her knees beside him, her hand on his face, her other hand tight in his, watching as his head tossed and turned and his muttering finally subsided.

"Baird?" Berneen's voice finally reached to him and he roused.

"Berneen? What?" He shifted his position, his hand reaching for hers, not realizing he already held her other hand.

"You were dreaming. At least, I think you were." She studied him, seeing the darkening bruises. "Who is Art?"

"Art? He was someone my Dad knew. Why?"

"Because you've mentioned him in your dreams."

Baird sighed, squinting at the clock, seeing Darby standing in the doorway, not sure where he needed to be. "Let me get up, and we'll talk."

She frowned at him. "You're not that strong yet, Baird."

"I'll manage. You go put on your tea and my coffee. Darby here can help me if I need help." He sighed as she refused to move. "Neen? I promise. I'll be careful."

Berneen stood for a moment, leaning back against the closed door, listening to the groans from Baird and the quiet comments from Darby, before she headed for the kitchen. Baird was right. They needed to talk. But they also needed to talk to Barnabas and whoever it was that was the leader of Baird's team. She knew the men were divided into two teams, but that they walked back and forth between the teams as necessary. That, Buckley had explained while they were captive.

She turned as she heard footsteps in the hall, leaning back on the fridge, watching carefully as Baird sank into a chair, Darby right behind him, hands held up in case Baird stumbled. He shared a look with his sister, shaking his head slightly. She sighed, knowing she was going to have to send for Doc, and not wanting to awaken him.

Their meal finished, Baird reached for the hands of the siblings, bowing his head for prayer. It took him a while to find his voice, emotions roiling within him. Darby studied his sister and her husband before he bowed his head, not sure what it all meant for them or where he fit in.

Chapter 15

Barnabas' fingers tapped against the papers Berneen had slid across the table to him. He watched her closely, not quite sure how to read her. He didn't know her well enough to do just that. His gaze shifted to Darby, finding him a hard read as well. Darby's eyes were on his sister and they were communicating in a silent manner. He then looked at Baird, a frown on his face as he watched his friend study his wife, a look in his eyes Barnabas had never seen before. He sighed even as he prayed, asking for safety for his friend.

"What is this, Berneen?" He flipped through the papers, not reading anything, as he waited for her answer.

She rubbed her hands along her legs, not sure how to even answer him. "It's names, dates, addresses. Anything Darby or I could think of." She turned her face to Baird, disconcerted to find him studying her so intently. "Baird has added some names and data as well."

"Baird?" Barnabas' voice finally cut through whatever or wherever Baird had drifted to and he looked up at his friend.

"Barnabas? What did you say?"

Barnabas ducked his head even as he shook it, to hide the grin he couldn't quite contain. Lord, I do believe my friend is falling in love right in front of me.

—

Bless these two, dear Lord. They have a lot to overcome.

"Baird? What exactly have you given me?" He looked down at the papers once more, a frown on his face. "What have you three gone and done?"

"Just listed names, addresses, dates, thoughts, whatever came up. We tried to organize it according to which one of us remembered what or who." Baird watched Barnabas closely, not quite sure if what they had done would help.

"This will help. Let me look through it and then we'll talk." Barnabas was soon engrossed in reading, his pen out marking spots on the pages, writing comments.

Baird shook his head, regretting it as it pounded. Berneen was on her feet, heading for the door as a knock came, and Doc walked in, a quiet word or two spoken to Berneen, before he was beside Baird, drawing him to his feet and back to the bedroom.

"How are you feeling, Baird? Don't try and hide it from me. You know you can't." Doc had his stethoscope out, ready to listen to the younger man's heart and lungs.

"I hurt, Doc, like I have never hurt in my life. I don't want Berneen to know how bad." Sweat beaded along his forehead as he spoke.

"She knows, Baird. She knows. You can't hide it from her. She's too perceptive." Doc turned as he heard a tap at the door and then Berneen slipped into the room.

"Doc? How is he?" Worry laced her voice.

"He's starting to heal, Berneen, but that will take time. Physically, that is. There are other emotions that he needs to deal with, that you need to deal with, and that as a couple you need to deal with." He stepped back, his eyes assessing the bruising. "The bruising is changing, Baird. You're healing. I would suggest you not go back to work before next week."

"I have to, Doc. I have plans I promised to have ready by Friday. I can't let that couple down."

Doc shook his head. "Just how far along are the plans?"

"Almost done. But then I have another couple coming in Friday afternoon to see me." Baird sighed, knowing what Doc would say. "I have to, Doc. I can't put them off."

"I'll allow it on one condition. Berneen there is with you." He held up a hand. "She's with you, calls me if she needs to, and you will rest when you can. Do you understand?"

Baird finally nodded. "I do, Doc, better than you think." He looked past Doc to where Berneen stood, hesitating as to what had been asked of her, emotions flowing across her face. He frowned for a moment. "Berneen?"

"Baird? Just what is it you do? I know you tutor and mentor youths from the local high school, but what your occupation is? That I have no idea. I won't agree to anything until you fully explain what you do." There was a bite to her words as she grew angry, not at

Baird, but at the circumstances that had joined their lives together and anger at the men who had caused it.

Doc shook his head. "You two need to talk. Baird's an architect, Berneen. He provides house drawings and plans, I think is how he words it, for low-income families and single people. He is paid by The Barnabas Foundation, as are all the men, but he does charge a nominal fee, which I understand goes back to the families once the house is built." His gaze steady on Berneen, he saw the moment she understood the character of the man sitting in front of her.

"Baird? Is this true?"

Baird sighed. "It is. Not many people know it, outside of the Foundation. That's how Barnabas has chosen to work it. I mean, they don't know that I am paid through the Foundation. That's confidential." He glared at Doc for a moment, who just laughed at him.

"She has to know, Baird. She has to know. And from what I understand, she now draws a salary from the Foundation as well, doesn't she?"

Berneen stared between the two men, finally remembering to snap her mouth closed. "No, that can't be right. I have to work. I have to support Darby and myself."

Baird rose, a hand resting on Doc's shoulder for a moment, before he walked to stand in front of Berneen. "That's what we have to talk about. I hadn't known how you felt. Barnabas can explain it. But yes, once we men marry, our wives draw a salary from the same source as we do. That's how Barnabas and his father wanted it. That way, we can both serve God where He wants us to be, whether in a work place or as a volunteer somewhere. We'll need to watch where you go for now. As for Darby, I imagine Barnabas has already taken steps to provide a source of income for him as well."

Berneen studied Baird, then looked past him at Doc, who was nodding, before her eyes slid closed and the tears she could not stop flowed down her face. She swiped at them angrily before she felt Baird just envelop her into his arms and hold her tight. She didn't hear Doc's quiet prayer before he walked from the room.

"Baird?"

"Neen? It's true. Barnabas will look after you two. And before you ask, it's okay. His father was a billionaire, investing over the years and just growing his finances. This is how he has chosen to use it, to help others out. It's part of how they see being a Barnabas, an encouragement."

She leaned back, to study him. "Just what do you mean, be a Barnabas? You all keep saying that, but not explaining it."

Baird wrapped an arm around her shoulders and led her from the room, heading for the kitchen, where he could heard Barnabas and Darby laughing over something Doc had said on his way out of the apartment.

"Barnabas? Have a moment? Can you explain what your Dad was thinking when he set up the Foundation? Berneen has asked." He slid back a chair

for her, seated her and then chose the chair beside her,
his hand coming out to grasp hers.

Chapter 16

Barnabas shot Baird a quick look before his gaze dropped to Berneen, seeing her confusion.

"Sure. You're a believer, I know, Berneen. You are familiar with Paul and his companion of his trips, Barnabas? Paul indicated that Barnabas was an encouragement to himself and other believers. Dad believed we needed people in today's world like Barnabas. He set up the Foundation, when I was born and named it for me, in order to do just that. The low-cost loans and grants helped out many. When he decided to retire and turned it over to me, we had a long, sometimes heated, discussion of where we wanted to go. He wanted to change the focus of it. I didn't. I wanted it to stay the way he had set it up. We finally came to see eye to eye on it. So, now our focus is mentoring, walking alongside those who are down and out, those who need a hand up. Do you understand?"

Berneen nodded, her eyes not having left Barnabas' face. "I do. I think it's wonderful. And why has no one else done this?" She shared a look with Darby, who had a slight frown on his face. "But I don't understand. Baird said that you had planned to provide an income for the wives as the guys married. Why?"

"Why? Because we want to. Because you ladies are worth more than the most precious jewel in the world. You will come in as helpmeets to my guys. It is only right that you have an income. You can work out in the work place, if you desire, or in volunteer situations. That is your choice. It makes no difference to your income." He turned to watch Darby, seeing the longing on the youth's face. "Darby, as of today, you have an income as well." He held up a hand as Darby went to protest. "No, it's only right. We need to help you out, to encourage you. You've had a rough life, both you and your sister. You are the people we look for to help."

"I wish you had been there years ago." Darby's broken words showed how deep his emotions ran before he was on his feet, heading for his room. They heard the door shut quietly behind him.

Berneen reached to hug Barnabas. "Thank you. You don't know what that means to Darby and to me. We've struggled for so long, making do with what I could manage to earn, going without so many things, even necessities."

Barnabas shared a look with Baird, before he spoke. "It's who we are, Berneen. All of us. We just want to help those who need it." He looked down at the papers in front of him as he heard her settle back against Baird, whose arm had come around her.

"Those names you wanted to take about, Barnabas?" Baird spoke, his eyes on Berneen.

"Those names. Yes. We need to talk about them." He sorted through the pages. "Berneen, Owen Small?"

"Him? That's a name I never wanted to hear again." She shivered, her arms wrapping tighter around herself

"Talk to me. Tell me about him." Barnabas pulled over a pad of paper and drew out his pen, catching Berneen's frown. "I work best with pen and paper. That's how I do it." He grinned at her before he sobered. "Who was he to you?"

"He was a lawyer Dad had used at work. Dad was a building inspector for the town over from here. He inspected commercial buildings. Small worked for the town, or so he said. Dad never was quite sure of him. He didn't have him do any personal work for him." She stared at Barnabas before she twisted to look up at Baird. "That's why I couldn't figure it out."

"Figure out what, Sweetheart?" Baird prompted her when she didn't speak for a few minutes.

"He said he was the lawyer Dad had used to draw up his will and his powers of attorney." She blinked back tears, her emotions still raw after all that time. "He told us the night after we buried Mom and Dad that we had to get out. That the house had been taken back over by the mortgage company and that Dad knew that was happening when he went overseas. He said he was Darby's guardian but he wanted nothing to do with the brat as he called him." She struggled with her anger. "He gave us thirty minutes to pack and leave. He dropped us off down town. I never knew

---

who to turn to. I didn't think I could go to the police. He told me that if I did, I would never see Darby again."

Barnabas' mouth had tightened as she spoke, knowing that she was repeating herself but also knowing she had to. "Do you know who your father used for personal legal matters?"

"I think it was Walter Trevor, but I can't be sure. I know he was a good friend of Dad's." She dropped her head to her hands. "I should have gone to him but I didn't."

"You were in shock. You were trying to look after yourself and your brother. I can have Brody approach him. He's the paralegal in the group. Is that okay?"

She nodded, her eyes thankful. "I guess. I should have but I was afraid."

"Afraid you'd lose Darby?" At her nod, Barnabas shook his head. "You were an adult at that point, right? There would have been no reason for them to take him away from you, unless it was played that you were homeless and incompetent to care for him." He looked at Baird as he drew in a deep breath.

"How wealthy were your parents, Berneen?" Baird's question had her turning her head once more to look at him.

"I'm not sure. We had a nice house, enough food, not extravagant, that I know. Dad was saving for our college funds, that's what he said."

Barnabas nodded. "Now, how did they die? And where?"

"They were in Europe. I'm not sure which country now. There was a riot and they were involved as bystanders. But I don't get it. They were the only ones hurt or killed. That doesn't sound right. It never did."

"We'll look into that as well." Barnabas paused as he flipped through the paperwork in front of him, pausing once in a while to read a sentence of paragraph. "Baird, your turn. Some of what you need to say, I know. But you have hidden depths that you have not told anyone, or if you have, it's been years."

Baird nodded, then sipped at his coffee, a grimace in place as he realized it had cooled. "We've talked many times, you and I, Barnabas, but you're right. There are things I have not said." He dropped his gaze to Berneen, who sat, leaning on his without realizing what she was doing, and waited for a moment, trying to gather his thoughts.

"Baird?" Barnabas' voice drew his attention and Baird sighed.

"Okay. So, where do I start?"

"Your mother, Baird?" Berneen had twisted once more so she could watch him. She saw Darby quietly taking a seat, knowing he needed to hear this as well.

—

Chapter 17

Baird drew a deep breath, knowing he needed to talk, had needed to for years. Lord, let me release this, please? You know I need to. Is this where I change to who You want me to be, to let go of baggage I've carried, baggage like that those I've mentored I've told to let go of?

He watched Darby closely, not sure how the youth would take what he had to say.

"Barnabas, you know my mother was killed in a bus accident when I was seven." He heard Berneen's softly indrawn breath and saw the tightened look that came across Darby's face. "Dad and I were a team, just the two of us. He was a commercial architect. I think he knew your father, Berneen, Darby, if he was a building inspector. I seem to remember a man named Dakin that he mentioned once or twice."

Berneen nodded. "He was. He inspected commercial buildings."

Baird continued. "Dad said there were some inspectors who were what he called 'shady', that took graft money. He knew your father didn't, Berneen. Somewhere he left a paper that named them all but I could never find it. Our house was searched after he died. I think that was what they were looking for."

Barnabas paused, his pen poised above the paper. "You never mentioned that your home was searched. Is there a police report?"

Baird nodded. "I have a copy. It happened when I was 19." He paused, working to control the anger he had felt at that invasion. "Dad was called to a commercial building. It wasn't one of his own, but the builder felt something was off and wanted a second opinion on it. He was there with Dad and a couple of other men. The building collapsed before they could get out. Shoddy workmanship was how the city termed it. I heard that a private investigator had been hired, but I never heard the outcome of that." He looked up at Barnabas. "I have notes that I can copy for you. We need to resolve this. Somehow I think this is all involved, Berneen's father, my Dad, and the lawyers."

"That's what the fellows are picking up. They know your father was clear, Berneen, Darby. They have determined he was not involved in any inspections of that building. And they know that your father was not the architect on record, Baird." Barnabas studied his notes. "Baird, what happened to all your belongings?"

Baird stiffened, sorrow on his face. "There was a fire about a month after Dad died. Everything was destroyed. It was always felt that it was arson, but no one ever confirmed that with me."

Barnabas nodded. "We'll look into that and pull reports as we can. Brody I think had come across that and was working on obtaining the reports he could." He paused as his phone chimed and he excused himself to take a call. He spun quickly as he listened, his eyes on Darby who had returned to sit beside his sister, their words quiet as they spoke to one another. He sighed as he pocketed his phone. Things just got more complicated, Lord. How do we solve this and keep these three safe at the same time? He was worried, he knew, not just for these three but for whoever else ended up in the path of the men who were after them.

Berneen watched him closely as he sat back down, her eyes thoughtful before they shifted to her brother, knowing somehow that whatever it was Barnabas had learned involved him.

"Barnabas?" Her quiet voice raised his head and he sighed once more.

"How close were you to the couple you were living with, Darby?" His question startled the siblings.

"They were people we knew through someone else. Why? What has happened to them?"

"They're safe. We moved them from their home after the guys found you." Barnabas watched Baird closely, knowing he had a good idea of where he was heading with his words. "But their house burned down last night. No one was inside, thank God."

"Burned down? How?" Darby shot to his feet, not sure if he should be heading for that couple or stay where he was.

"We're talking with the arson investigator now and the investigating officer. We'll know more." Barnabas pointed to the chair. "Sit, Darby. They're safe. We moved them and all their possessions out of there last night."

"You did? How?"

Barnabas gave a quick grin. "We had friends, more than we really needed, who went in, packed them up, and moved them. I won't tell you where they are but they are safe. They were worried about you and Berneen."

Darby sat back. "But how did they know where I was?"

"That we're working on as well. Branigan would like to see your backpack, if he can. They may have slipped something in there to track you."

Darby was on his feet and back with the pack. "Do you need anything that was in it?"

"Not at the moment, but Branigan may want to look it over, only if it's okay with you and Berneen."

"Do what you need to, Barnabas. I want this over." Berneen's voice once more had a bite to it, drawing Darby's eyes to his sister. He was not used to the tone of voice she was using.

'We'll do our best to keep you both safe, you and Darby, Berneen."

"But will it be enough?" She was on her feet and they heard the sliding door to the balcony open and close.

"Baird? You're off to work?" Barnabas' change of subject brought Darby's eyes to him.

"I am. Branigan's with me. That's the condition Doc put on me going back."

"Then, I guess, Darby, you're with me. Come on. I'll show you around and introduce you to some of the men who may be around. I know Doc's Anna will be looking for you. She's told me that." Barnabas gathered his papers, rose and then followed Darby from the room, his heart raising in prayer for Baird, knowing they were not done, not by a long shot, he thought, with the men after them. They really hadn't figured it out yet, either, and that worried him more than he let on.

Chapter 18

A cup of her tea in her hand, Berneen wandered Baird's office, her fingers coming out once in a while to trace a picture, a portrait, a model. She could see the intensity he put into his work, the desire to provide the best he could for those who were less well off. She finally turned, perching against a credenza and watched as he work, his concentration on the drawing he was finishing off, seeing the ruffled curls he had been running his fingers through. She also saw the pain on his face and sighed. It was time for him to take a break and just how did she get him to do that?

She walked quietly back into the reception area, studying the desk there, knowing he worked on his own without a secretary. She sat for a moment, her eyes searching the desk, before she rose and walked over to a canvas of Lake Erie at its wildest, she thought. She looked for the artist name and could not find it. She stepped back a bit, her mind searching through the Scriptures about storms, and feeling a calmness and peace come over her. God, You're here, right in the midst of my storm. You are here. I am not alone. I don't need to fear the storm. You can calm the waves, the wind, the rain. But You can and do bring peace to me. Thank you.

She felt an arm come around her and then leaned back against Baird. She was slowly learning to trust him, even though it had only been a few days she had known him. She realized she had read his character correctly when they had both been captive first.

"Are you ready to go, Baird?"

"Almost. You seem entranced with that photo."

"I am. I was just remembering verses about God and storms. We're in the middle of a huge one, I think."

"That we are, but we are not alone, never alone." He waited for her to ask about the artist. "I took that just after Dad died. It suited my mood at the moment."

"It's beautiful, Baird. I can see why you would say what you just did about it." She looked down at his hands lightly grasping hers and frowned again, studying the engraved red gold ring on his finger and then the matching band on hers. "Baird?"

"Yes, Sweetheart?"

"The rings. Who picked them out?"

"I did. They had picked out plain thin gold rings. I didn't like them."

"And how hard a time did you have?" She felt him shrug. "Do you think they had placed something in them to track us?"

"That's what I guess I was thinking. I was also thinking that a plain gold band didn't suit you. You needed something more, something special."

She sighed once more as she leaned back on him, feeling him sway slightly. "Thank you. Now, are you done enough that you can leave?"

"I am. I need to check my messages, though." He released her and moved to the reception desk, sliding heavily into it.

"Teach me how to check them. I can do that. I can't just sit here and do nothing." Berneen was at his side, perching on the corner of the desk. "Please, Baird? I need to feel useful. I haven't felt needed or wanted in months."

"Darby needs you." He sat back, his eyes on her downcast face. "I need you, Berneen. I don't think you realize how much."

She shook her head, not looking at him, sliding from the desk. "No, you don't. You just think you do. Come on, Baird. You need your medications, don't you?" She walked through the door, not looking back, leaving Baird staring after her, sorrow on his face, but also determination to show her exactly how much she was needed.

Lord, I'm falling in love with her, even in such a short time, and I have no idea where to go with that. I don't know how she feels and I won't ask. She'll need to tell me, if and when she is ready to. Even if it takes fifty years, I won't leave her.

He rose, feeling the pain but not as bad as he had. He healed quickly, he knew, and prayed that this time, he would heal even quicker. He turned out the lights, closed and locked the door behind him, and then reached for Berneen's hand, not catching her look at him or their linked hands.

Breck watched the couple walk away, then down at the papers in his hands. He needed to talk to

Berneen, but shrugged, walking back to his own office, not willing to disturb them at that time. He would catch up with them later. He looked up to see Darby standing in front of him, a forlorn, lost look on his face.

"Darby? Looking for me?"

Darby shrugged. "I don't know. I just need to be doing something and don't know what. I've managed to get through that pile of homework someone left for me." He grinned at Breck. "Thank you for talking to my teachers. I can keep up with the class now."

Breck shrugged off Darby's thanks and then dropped the papers on his desk before he turned Darby around. "Come on. Have we shown you our gym? It even has a walking track and when the weather is cold, we have an outdoor rink. Play hockey?"

"Shinny. I do. Say, this is great!" Darby's face glowed at the thought of playing shinny, a favourite sport of his. "Do you guys play hockey or shinny?"

"We do, as much as we can. Barnabas is in the planning stages for a rink near the edge of the property that can be used by community groups. We get to use it anytime it's free, when it's finished."

Chapter 19

Keeping his eyes on Berneen seated on the couch, Baird reached for the papers Breck was endeavouring to get her to take.

"They won't bite, Berneen." Breck grinned at the dark look she shot him. "Just some paperwork to complete. Routine stuff."

"Routine stuff. That's what they all say before they ask for a complete life history on you. Why?"

"Why? Because we need this for you. You're part of our family now and we need to put data on file for you. If not for our records, then for the government's."

"Right. The good old government. The government that never helps." Berneen knew she was grumbling but couldn't stop herself.

Breck shook his head. "Just complete them and get them back to me, please? It's likely nothing more than what you would complete for employment and likely a lot less. Name. Address. Both of which we do know. And banking information so we can begin to deposit your cheques."

"Can I refuse that?"

Breck stared at her, shocked before he looked at Baird, who was shaking his head. "Refuse the cheques? Berneen, did Barnabas not explain what is laid out in our charter? That when the men marry, their wives collect earnings from us?"

"He did. I'm just not sure on that." She was being obstinate, she knew, just why, she wasn't sure.

"It doesn't matter if you're sure or not. It goes into your account. You are now an employee of the Foundation." He rose, disappointment on his face. "You're the first one of the guys' wives. Don't let what you've been through colour how you look on what we do or what we provide." He walked away, the door closely quietly behind him.

Baird stared at her for a moment, then walked away, leaving her on her own, her thoughts jumbled and dark. She wasn't up to this, she thought. She didn't deserve any of this. Then, she heard a small voice speaking to her, telling her that God had seen what she had been through, that He had been there with her, and that He had planned this for her. All she had to do was accept it. But could she? That was the question she couldn't answer. She reached for the papers Breck had dropped on the chair and then searched for a pen, filling out what she needed to.

She hadn't heard Baird for a bit and went looking for him, finally finding him in his home office, stretched out on the couch, sound asleep. Covering him with the afghan that lay on the back of the chair, she slipped to a sitting position beside him, her hand on his face, wincing at the various colours that showed, knowing she owed him her life. She was aware that she not likely would have survived much longer her captivity.

———

101

She rose, heading for the outside door, Breck's papers in her hands, stopping for a moment to stare back down the hallway, not sure if this was where she was meant to be. All she knew was that she felt safe and secure, even though danger still swirled around her.

Breck watched Berneen closely as she paced his office, her papers dropped in front of him.

"Berneen? What's up? It's not about this, is it?" He tapped the papers.

"No, it's not. I'm just so confused. Does that make sense? I mean, I feel safe. I feel secure. I know you all will look out for me. I have Darby back with me. But I feel as if I'm in a holding pattern, not able to move forward, certainly not backwards. That there is danger ahead, not just for me, but for Baird, Darby and all of you."

Breck nodded. "It's all that, Berneen. You have had to make a major decision in your life, to save someone else and yourself. You have been living on the edge for too many years, not able to grieve for your parents, raising Darby since he was what five? You have not been able to do things a young lady should have been able to do. Now, you find yourself in a situation where danger is all around you, and you don't know who or why. That, we are working on."

"Have you found out anything at all? Why would they want me to stay with Baird all the time? That doesn't make sense."

Breck motioned to a chair and waited until she had seated herself. "It does, if what we're looking at is true. We're thinking revenge of some kind."

"Revenge?" Her voice rose and she clapped her hands over her mouth. "Revenge? But why? Who?"

"We're looking at the original architect on the building that collapsed on Baird's Dad. At the men who were with him. Their relatives. Friends. Business associates." He looked down for a moment before looking back at her. "At your parents. Who they knew. Who your Dad worked with." He held up a hand as she went to speak. "Just bear with me for a moment, please?" He thought quickly through what he knew. "We know for sure that your parents were murdered. We have that documentation from overseas. Why it was never followed up on here, we are working through that. It appears that the reports ended up on an investigator's desk, and he just buried them."

"He buried them? You mean, this could all have been solved years ago and maybe I wouldn't have had to do this? Wouldn't have had to live pay cheque to pay cheque and that not well at all?"

"That's possible, Berneen. We're working with the new investigator. He's heading overseas tomorrow to see what he can learn."

She just shook her head. "But you really don't know who or why, do you?" She was on her feet, running from his office, leaving him to come after her.

Breck watched as Baird stopped her, his arms around her as she struggled to escape his embrace.

Baird just tightened his hold, his eyes on Breck as he approached.

"Breck? What happened? I woke up, found Berneen not there, and came looking for her."

"She brought me her paperwork, but she didn't like the fact the original investigator had the documents from overseas and didn't investigate anything." He looked down at Berneen, who by this time had calmed enough to stand still in Baird's embrace. "We have definite word that they were murdered. It was a set up, Baird, and we don't know why or who, or how it affects Berneen and Darby. Not yet, anyway."

Berneen shoved herself away from Baird, a dark look on her face. "How do I tell Darby?"

Breck looked behind the couple, a sigh rising but not released. "I think he knows, Berneen. He's right behind you."

Berneen spun, her eyes on her brother, seeing the devastation on his face before she moved to him, hugging him tight, feeling the tears he shed, knowing he didn't want her to see them.

Chapter 20

A blanket tucked around her, a pillow beside her, Berneen curled up in a corner of the couch, a tablet of paper in front of her, pen tapping quietly. She had left only the lamp beside her on, knowing that if there were more lights, either one of the men in her life might come and send her to bed, and she just wasn't ready to sleep. She had made the rounds of the two bedrooms, finding both Baird and Darby asleep. She brushed at the hair that had escaped her braid, not realizing what she was doing, it was just a habit.

She stared at the paper, knowing she needed to start working through her memories, and not sure if she was ready for that, if she ever would be. Her pen finally began to move, as she wrote paragraph after paragraph, stopping every once in a while to ease the cramp in her hand. She stared at the conclusion she had come to. No, she thought. No him or her! Why?

She didn't hear the soft footsteps on the hardwood floor heading her way until the papers were gently removed from her hands and dropped to the table in front of the couch. Hands shifted her so that Baird could stretch out beside her, her pillow tucked behind him, the blanket covering them, her body cradled in his arms, her head on his shoulder. She started for a moment and then relaxed.

"You need to sleep, Sweetheart." Baird's quiet voice was barely audible.

"I can't. I need to solve this."

"No, you need to sleep. Darby said you only sleep for an hour or two at a time and are then up wandering around."

"I thought I hid that from him." She twisted her head to look up at Baird. "You need to shave."

He gave a light laugh. "And here I thought the beard would cover the bruising. Guess not, eh?" He tucked the blanket tighter around her. "Darby knows you're not sleeping. He told me he's known for years. He's that worried about you he couldn't not share with me."

She dropped her face back against him. "I didn't know. I thought he was sleeping when I was up." She yawned, fatigue suddenly hitting her hard. "I figured out who it is. I wouldn't have suspected them."

"Did you? Care to share?" Baird waited and then realized she was asleep. He reached for her papers, careful not to disturb her and flipped through them, his breath catching as he saw who she had named. Lord, why now? Why did she come to this conclusion? It is going to be hard to prove, but You know where the proof is. Just protect my lady and my sweetheart, please, dear Lord? I don't want her hurt, not again. He too slept, what he cared for most in the world tight in his arms.

Darby walked quietly through the house a few hours later, surprised at finding Baird's door open. He squinted at the clock on the microwave, noting it was only five in the morning. He saw the low light in the living room and stopped in the arched doorway, his eyes on his sister, before he looked at Baird. He had heard Baird moving around the apartment about midnight. He sighed, praying that his sister had slept for longer than her normal. She needs it, Lord. Baird is good for her. He challenges her without putting her down. She's had that enough, been driven to her knees in more ways than one, and that not always to pray. He turned, heading for his bedroom, quietly shutting the door and reaching for his Bible. He felt the danger around them and desperately needed to feel safe. When or how that would happen, he had no idea, but he needed to find solace in the Scriptures. That was what Berneen had taught him.

Baird finally roused, his eyes on his watch, before he looked down at Berneen, who still slept, her hand clutching his T-shirt tightly. He touched her hair lightly before he moved, sliding away from her and upright, reaching to tuck the blankets around her. He walked away, finding Darby in the kitchen, blinking at the daylight coming in the window.

"Darby? You're up?"

"Well, yeah! It is after eight after all. I thought you had to be in the office by ten."

Baird nodded. "I do." He looked back at the living room. "Berneen's still asleep."

"She is? That's unusual. She never sleeps like that." Darby rose to pour Baird's coffee, setting the mug in front of the older man. "How long?"

"About seven hours or more I would say."

"You're good for her, Baird. She needs you in her life." Darby looked down, blinking back tears. "So do I."

"I don't plan on leaving anytime soon, not if I can help it. That I promise you." Baird finished his coffee and rose. "I was told I needed to shave. Let your sister sleep. If she's not awake when I have to leave, can you stay with her?"

"I can. I have some studying to do." Darby searched Baird's face. "What did she do?"

"She came up with some names. I need to pass them on to the guys. I can do that later." Baird walked away, not seeing the look on Darby's face.

Chapter 21

Branigan stared at Baird as he slumped in his desk chair, worn out from his conference with the new clients, before his eyes dropped to the papers Baird had just handed him.

"She did what?"

"She named a couple of people she thinks are responsible. I have no idea how she came up with them. I just scanned through her notes. That's a copy. I couldn't take the originals. I needed to leave them with her." He nodded at the papers. "I saw who she's named. I would never have suspected them. Now, how do we prove what she's come up with?"

"Your lady has a very scary mind, Baird." Branigan slid down into a chair as he read through her notes. "She's good. Very concise. Gives facts. Provides suppositions and questions. Gives a very clear reason for why she suspects who she does." He looked up and then around as he heard footsteps and Berneen appeared in the doorway, worry on her face.

"Baird? When did you come down here? I couldn't find you."

Baird was on his feet, drawing her to him and then down to his chair with him as he seated himself again. "Didn't Darby tell you?"

"Darby? He knew? He left a note that he was away with Benen and Bradon." She looked up then, and flushed, seeing Branigan watching them, a smile on his face. "Branigan? I'm sorry. I didn't know you were here."

"That's okay, Berneen. I was just leaving. Baird has taken the opportunity to pass on your thoughts. We'll be working on them."

She stared, open mouthed, as he walked away. "Baird? What did you do?"

"Gave him a copy of your notes. You know we needed to do that. Now. About us."

"What about us?" She twisted in his arms. "Have you solved the mystery yet?"

"Not quite. I just was wondering if I could take you out for a meal."

She gaped at him. "Baird! How can we? It's not safe!"

"We also can't hide." He didn't put into words his thoughts, that if they were out and about, just maybe they could draw out the ringleaders, have them arrested, and solve this so they could go on with their lives.

Berneen rose, shaking her head. "Absolutely not. We are not going out in the open."

Baird rose as well, staring down at her. "We can't hide forever. You can if you want. I don't intend to." He walked away, heading for the room he kept his samples of materials in.

Berneen watched and then fled, tears on her cheeks. Anna saw her coming, stopped her and then swept her into an empty room.

"Berneen? What is going on?" Anna's hug was welcoming before she seated Berneen and drew up a chair, her hands reaching for the younger woman's.

"Baird wants to take me out somewhere. I don't think it's safe. He can't be hurt again because of me." Berneen refused to look up until Anna's hand under her chin raised her face.

"Berneen, what are you really afraid of? Being left on your own again? Losing Darby too?" Anna's voice held compassion as she prayed for the younger woman.

Berneen finally nodded. "I am. I don't want anyone else hurt." She stared at Anna, grief on her face. "I don't think I had a chance to grieve for Mom and Dad, things happened too quickly and too harshly."

"And now it's all coming out, all these emotions, a new living situation. A husband you never expected to ever have, one who wants to cherish you and treat you as you should be treated." Anna sat back, her hands folded in her lap. "Baird has never dated, has shown no desire to get to know any of the young women who throw themselves at him. We see how he watches you, even in such a short time that we've known you. He treats you as a lady should be treated. He treats you as an important part of his life. I know Baird well enough to know that even if you decide to move on, seek an annulment, and leave him, he will never marry again. It's not who he is. However you two managed to come together as a couple, forced as it was, he is determined to protect you and prove to you that you are a person of value, someone who he would like to get to know, to be that important part of your life. He knows what he was asking when he wanted to take you out for a meal. He knows the danger you would face. He's willing to take that risk. Are you?"

Anna's eyes raised as she heard the footsteps stop at the doorway and saw Baird standing there, heart on his face, his eyes on Berneen. Berneen didn't raise her eyes from Anna's face, her mind working with what Anna had said. She drew a quivering breath, not sure how she wanted to proceed, if she even did. She had not been asked if she wanted to marry Baird. She had been given little choice, that she knew. She had known she could not have his death on her hands and that's what would have happened.

She shook her head. "I'm so confused, Anna. So confused." She bent over, her face covered by her hands. "I need to talk to someone but I don't know who."

Anna's hand rested on Berneen's head. "You do, love. I would have suggested Buckley in other circumstances, but he's too close to the situation. The best person to talk to is Baird. And I'm not sure that you're ready to do just that. Are you?" She felt the slight shrug Berneen gave. "How can we help you, Berneen?" She moved back as Baird approached, dropping to his knees beside Berneen, his arms going around her.

———

"Neen? Don't cry. Please. Let's talk. I'm okay with not going out to dinner, if you're that worried about it."

Berneen turned to watch Baird, finding his face close to hers. She was torn, not sure what to do, wanting to trust, but not sure if she could.

"Can you trust me, Neen?" He watched her face, seeing subtle signs of the struggle she was going through that she refused to let him know about. "Don't hide from me, please? Let me walk through this with you. You need someone there."

She finally leaned into him, her voice broken as she spoke. "I want to, Baird. I really want to, but it's been so long. Too long, I think. I haven't been able to trust anyone but myself to keep Darby and I safe. It's hard to let go of that."

"We know, Sweetheart. We know." He stood, pulling her to her feet, walking towards Anna. "Anna, I think a shopping trip is in order. Are you game?"

"About time, is what I think. I'm game. In fact, Blair and Brady are waiting out front for us."

Berneen's eyes grew huge. "They are? Why?"

"Just because. They want a trip to town and want you and I and Baird to go with them."

Baird snorted. "Yeah, right. As if they need us."

"But, you see, Baird, they do. They want to make sure you and Berneen can get out and this is their way of saying welcome to the family, Berneen."

Berneen stopped, bringing the two with her to a halt. "It is? Why?"

"Because you are a part of the family. This is where part of your desire to trust comes in. Baird knows these men, he works with them. They know Baird. They are getting to know your brother. He's not letting them away with not getting to know him. They want to know the woman who has captured Baird's heart." Anna walked away from them at that point, heading for the outside door.

Baird watched the changes that flickered across Berneen's face, the emotions, and saw the instant that she gave in and then reached for his hand.

"I guess, then, Baird, we're off to town."

Chapter 22

Two days later, Berneen watched as Baird walked back towards her from the rear of the church parking lot. He had driven them to church, the church Buckley pastored, and she was not sure she should be there. He reached for her hand, his eyes thoughtful as he studied the building.

"You don't want to go in, do you, Baird?" Darby asked the obvious question.

"It's not that, Darby. It's your sister I'm concerned about. This is so sudden. No announcements or anything of what was coming. I'm not sure the people will understand."

Darby stopped walking, his hand out to stop Baird. "Will they judge her, condemn her?"

Baird shrugged. "I have no idea. I am sure some will. We'll try and keep it as low key as we can. That's why we're coming in almost at time for the service to start. The other guys will be around us. We leave before the last song. We're trying to keep your sister safe, and I'm not sure that we can."

"We don't have to go, Baird, if it's that much work." Berneen tried to back away, but Baird just swept an arm around her and nudged her forward.

"It's no work. We always sit together at the back, all of us, except for Barnabas. He's usually up front. So there's no problem. Six of them and Darby will be in the row in front of us. We'll do our best to keep you safe." He looked around, feeling eyes watching them, not seeing anyone that stood out, but knowing at that moment just how much of a risk they were taking. He urged the siblings into the church and then to the pew they would sit in, timing it so that they entered as the congregation was standing for the first song.

Berneen sat, fascinated as she listened to the sermon Buckley brought, a sermon about learning to trust. She shivered every once in a while and glanced behind her, knowing someone was watching her.

"Someone's there?" Baird low question caught her attention.

"There is, but I don't know who." She looked up at him and then across the aisle to the other side of the church, finding curious eyes on her with no condemnation shown.

"Buckley's almost finished and then we'll go." Baird rose, caught her hand and led her from the church, his team members surrounding them until Baird had closed the door to his car, after seating her in the passenger seat.

"Did you see anyone?" Baird's eyes searched each of the five men.

"No one that we would suspect. But then, she's named people we would never have suspected." Benen spoke, his voice low as he searched the area. "Let's get you two home again. I don't like the feeling I'm getting."

"Me neither." Brady headed for his vehicle, Benen beside him. The other three men would follow in Branigan's vehicle.

Berneen watched as they pulled away from the church. "Is this really necessary? Isn't it overkill?"

Baird shook his head. "No, it's not. Branigan got a text message during the service from one of our security guards. They received a direct threat aimed at you. They plan something today. We need to get you home and safe."

Berneen stared at him before she shifted in her seat to stare out the side window. "This is too much, Baird. When does it end? Darby?"

"He's safe. They won't try for him unless they can't get to you. The other team knows what's up and will take precautions." He glanced at her as he parked in his designated spot and laid a hand on her arm. "Wait until the other guys are here. We'll go in together."

She shuddered, a sudden chill running through her. "We can't do this all the time, Baird. There are times when we'll be on our own or out together without them." She turned once more, a thought crossing her mind. "Do they know if we're not together all the time? And just what did they mean by that?"

"That's what we're working through. I think Barnabas was correct when he said revenge. This is what it feels like. The not knowing. The worry. The fear. The uncertainty. We don't know when or why they'll hit."

"That's what I don't get. I was held against my will. There were at least four men they brought in before you. Those men disappeared. They were only there for a couple of days. But now that I think of it, I'm not sure they were even prisoners. They could have been part of the gang, brought in to terrorize me."

Baird stared at her before he was out of the car, yanking open her door, and running with her towards the building.

"Baird? What on earth?"

He led her to his office, unlocking the door, shoving her down into a chair, before he turned to the five men who had followed them. "I think Berneen just solved part of the puzzle."

"How so?" Benen reached for the coffee pot and headed for the kitchenette, knowing that it would be needed. "Berneen? Do you want some of your tea?"

She was on her feet, brushing by Baird to help Benen. "I do. I can't sit still and be waited on."

"Baird? Care to explain your comment?" Blair opened up a package of food Anna had handed him earlier that day, knowing that they would likely want something.

"Berneen commented that the men that were brought in may have been part of the gang."

Branigan nodded as he sorted through the mugs, setting out utensils that might be needed. "That's what we're beginning to think. That this was all a ploy, Baird, and that you were the one they wanted there all along. Why? As we've decided, revenge. It's the only answer. But who? That's the question. We think it's the family of one of the men who died when your Dad did.   But we haven't got enough evidence or information to go to the police. Berneen? We'll need you to work through your captivity. I don't think anyone has had you go over it in a detailed manner."

"No, we haven't." She stood, leaning against a door frame, her mug in her hand, her eyes on Branigan. "That's what we need to do." She moved to set her mug down, but Brady's hand stopped her. "Brady?"

"First we eat, Berneen. We'll get to your observations in a bit." He pulled out a chair and shoved her down, grinning at her comment of bossy men and why did she need them anyway?

Baird had stepped back, his eyes on Berneen and his friends, watching how they interacted. He could see that she was relaxing around them, her attention on something other than trying to be herself around them. He raised his eyes, meeting Branigan's eyes, who nodded.

Chapter 23

Berneen listened closely as Baird interacted with his friends and team mates. She could see and feel the trust the men had for one another. She turned as Bradon sat down beside her, Kade nudging at her arm for attention.

"Bradon? You have a puzzled look on your face."

He nodded. "I do. I've read over what you wrote. I just don't get how the lawyer managed to get away with this."

"I was eighteen, Bradon, in shock, grieving. I had a five-year-old brother I was trying to comfort and keep everything as close to normal for him as I could. I didn't know any better." She bit back the anger she was beginning to feel. "I never had a chance to look through any paperwork. I know Dad had a safe and he gave me the combination to it, but we were out of the house before I could even do that." She blinked back the tears of frustration and anger that prickled at her eyes.

"We get that, Berneen. Believe me, we get that. But do you know if the house was sold or not?"

She stared at him. "I have no idea. Dad always said it couldn't be sold. That it was to be a family home for as long as there were descendants. Can we look into that?"

He grinned and pulled his laptop over to him. "We can and we will. Now, the address." He typed rapidly as she spit it out, Baird having come to stand behind her, his hands on her shoulders. "There. Now, let's see." Bradon perused various articles, clicking rapidly through screens.

Berneen watched, envy growing inside her as she watched how he maneuvered his laptop with ease.

"We'll get you a laptop, Sweetheart, and we'll teach you to use it." Baird spoke quietly in her ear.

"You will? I can? I never had a chance. We didn't have the money for extras. Darby is learning at school, but other than the cash register at work, I don't know computers." She groaned. "Work! I never thought, Baird. I need to talk to them. I left them in the lurch." She was becoming upset, and the men in the room hesitated in their work to study her and then Baird.

Baird dropped to a crouch beside her, an arm around her, as he shared a look with Bradon. "We can do that. I have to work tomorrow morning, but in the afternoon, we can head to town and you can pick out your very own lap top. And we can call your work or you can go in, whichever is the easiest for you."

Her hand touched his face lightly and then her attention was drawn to a photo on Bradon's computer. "That's my home. It looks the same. What year?"

"That was taken a month ago, from what I am reading. The comments are that there has been no one living in it for years, but the taxes and utilities are paid.

———

The town can't do anything about that." He sat back, a frown on his face as he rubbed the back of his neck. "That's strange. You were told the house had been forfeited, but no one is living there." He looked around. "We need Brody. He has sites he can search that we don't have access to."

Brady was out the door, running through the hallways, finding Brody as he was heading up the stairs.

"Brody? Do you have a few minutes?" Brady slid to a halt, a hand on the wall to balance himself.

"I do. Why?"

"Because we've found Berneen's old home on the internet. She was told it was forfeited. Bradon has found evidence that it's not. We need you to research for us, if you've time."

Brody walked rapidly back the way Brady had come. "Where are you working? Baird's office?"

"We are. Anna sent in food, if you haven't eaten."

"I have." He stopped in the doorway, assessing what was happening before he moved to a chair beside Bradon. "Bradon? Talk to me."

"Brody, you know that Berneen was told her home was forfeited. But it doesn't seem that it was. I found evidence in a newspaper article from a month ago that it is still being cared for, taxes and utilities paid. This is strange."

Brody nodded, then with a question on his face, reached for Bradon's laptop. "May I?"

Bradon motioned with his hands. "Go ahead. This is part of the puzzle we need to solve." He rose and stepped away, turning back to watch Berneen and then looking up as Darby found his sister.

Darby's quiet words to his sister had her sitting back and staring at him.

"You're sure, Darby?" At his nod, she sighed. "This just makes it worse, doesn't it? When did you find out?"

"Just now." He thrust a phone at her that he had been holding. "Baird gave me this. I haven't given the number to anyone but the couple I was staying with. Someone is trying to find them. They're looking for me, Berneen. How do they stay safe?"

Baird looked around Berneen at him. "They're safe, Darby. We have them tucked away where they can't be found."

"Are you sure, Baird?" Darby was worried but trying hard not to how it.

"Trust me, Darby. Barnabas has made sure of that." He looked around at a sound from Brody. "Brody?"

Brody's eyes rose from where he had been studying a website. "This is worse than we thought, Baird. Far worse."

Chapter 24

All eyes were on Brody as he spoke, before Baird stood and walked to stand behind him, his eyes on the laptop screen.

"What did you find out?" Baird could see Berneen reach for Darby and grasp his hand.

"Someone has tried to change the ownership on the house, tried to change the name the utilities are in. Apparently a copy of a will was presented, but it didn't match the documentation on file." Brody looked around at Baird. "I have a name, but I'm not sure if it's correct."

"Who is it?" Berneen's voice was tight, her hand gripping Darby's just as tightly.

"Owen Small. He's not the attorney that your father put on record, though."

Berneen gave a harsh laugh. "He's the one who chased us from that home." She rose, coming to stand beside Baird, not conscious of how his arm encircled her. "Can we get into the house?"

"I don't see why not. According to the record here, you're listed as the owner, with Darby listed as a minor, to become part owner at age 18." Brody looked over at Darby as he made a sound. "You never knew, Darby?"

Darby shook his head, as he walked to stand beside his sister, his eyes on the family home. "No. I don't know that we ever discussed that. Did we, Berneen?"

"We didn't, not that I remember. I thought if the house was gone, there was no point." She stared at her brother. "I'm sorry, Darby. I should have fought harder to keep you there."

"I don't think you had much choice, Berneen. Not from what you've said." Brody pointed at an article he had pulled up. "It says here that Small had taken over your father's office and was removed forcibly by the authorities. They are still trying to find evidence that he has hidden about his activities."

"It will be hidden in the house somewhere. Would he have changed the locks?" Berneen began to pace, not sure where she was going with her questions, only certain that she wanted back into her home.

Branigan shared a look with Baird before he spoke. "I do security systems, Berneen. As such, I am a trained locksmith. I'll get you into your house. Do we have what we need in documentation, Brody?"

"We should do. I'll talk to the police tomorrow morning. We need to get in there as soon as we can."

Late that evening, Baird clicked off the kitchen light and, coffee mug in hand, he headed for the living room, settling down into his favourite recliner, feet up, and watched Berneen silently as she huddled on the couch, wrapped in a blanket, her eyes on the floor in front of her. He didn't think she was looking at anything in particular, but he was hesitant to speak. He finally sighed, set aside his mug of coffee, and moving to the couch, he swept her into his arms, settling back where she had been sitting and wrapping the blanket around them. His feet went up on the table, and his head tilted so he could watch her face.

"Neen? Talk to me. You haven't said much said Brody found the picture of your house."

She shook her head. "What can I say, Baird? What is there to say?"

He heard the defeat in her voice. "It's not your fault, Neen. You didn't know. You were too young."

"I still should have known. I should have checked it out. I should have gone to the police." Her head dropped to his shoulder as her anger abated. "It's not fair, Baird. Just not fair. So much has been taken from Darby."

"And from you. Ssh. Sleep, Neen. Brody will let us know tomorrow when we can get it." He dropped a kiss on her hair, not even realizing he had done so, and rested his cheek against her head.

Berneen stilled, feeling the kiss, a wonder starting to move in her heart, softening the hardness she had worked to install in it, not willing to love again.

"Who hurt you so bad, Neen?" Baird's quiet question was unexpected. He didn't think she would answer, she just wasn't ready to trust him that far, not with her heart at any rate.

She shrugged, then yawned, her eyes closing as she slept. Baird waited and then slept himself, shifting to a more comfortable position.

Darby squinted at the clock hours later as he made his way to the kitchen, not surprised to find

Berneen in the living room, but when he saw Baird, he stopped, the slight noise of his socked feet on the floor rousing Baird.

"Darby? You up?"

Darby snorted before he grinned. "Considering it's morning, then yeah, I'm up."

"What time is it?" Baird shifted, his eyes on Berneen as she still slept.

"After six. Didn't you say you had to be in your office by eight?"

"I do." Baird yawned but made no effort to move.

Darby shook his head as he reached for Baird's cup of cold coffee. "I'll make fresh." He studied his sister, then spoke once more. "Thanks, Baird."

Baird twisted his neck, working at the stiffness, as he watched Darby. "For what?"

"For being you. For taking me in when you didn't have to. For that." Darby nodded at his sister.

"For what?" Baird repeated himself.

"For that. She doesn't trust easily, if at all. To see her sleeping like that? I don't think she's slept more than an hour or two at a time for the last ten years. Thank you." Darby walked away, his shoulders hunched as he tried to control his emotions.

"You're welcome, Darby. You're family. This is what family does." Baird shifted Berneen away from him, rose, and then watched as she settled back down on the couch, a slight smile on her face, before he tucked the blanket around her once more. He stood, watching her, feeling the ice in his heart melting more. He shook his head and then headed for his shower, rubbing at his face, noting the pain was less and the swelling was going down. He wouldn't scare the clients too much, he thought.

Chapter 25

Watching Berneen intently, Brody moved through the group of men towards where she stood with Baird and Darby, uncertainty on her face. Brody glanced around, seeing Branigan talking with the officers on hand before he glanced at the tidy grounds surrounding the two-story house they all stood in front of. It was Tuesday afternoon, and all fourteen men had taken the time to be there, to support Baird, but more importantly, to support Berneen and Darby.

"Brody?" Baird's quiet voice barely broke through the stillness surrounding them. He glanced around, seeing neighbours on their porches, curious as to what was happening.

"We're almost ready to go in. We'll let the officers go in first with Branigan. Then, we'll walk you through." He peered closely at Berneen as he spoke, seeing the tension, fear, anxiety and whatever emotions she was feeling flickering on her face. Darby just stood, his eyes on the house, not sure how he felt. It had been too long, and he had been too young.

Berneen gave an abrupt nod, her eyes intent on the officers as they moved towards the front door, watching in amazement as Branigan used the key she had handed him to unlock the door. For some reason, she had never been able to throw the key away, bringing in out in the darkness of the night, to feel it in sorrow and grief, to clench it in anger. She lost track of the number of times she had pitched into a garbage can only to go back and dig it out, tucking it away in a pocket. She moved slightly, her hand tucked tight in Baird's, her other hand tight in Darby. She turned her head to watch Darby, finding interest on his face but not the emotions she was feeling.

"Darby?"

Darby turned his head to study his sister, seeing the emotions she was endeavouring to cover. "It's okay, Neen. I'm okay. But you? Are you?"

She shrugged, her eyes going back to the open front door. "No, I don't think I am. I have no idea what we'll find, what he has done inside. It's almost too hard, Darb." She spun suddenly, seeking solace in Baird's arms, realizing as she did so that she had learned to trust him in a way she hadn't trusted anyone before.

Baird's arms held his bride tight, his chin on the top of her head, before he reached out an arm and swept Darby into a hug as well. Darby leaned against Baird, realizing he now had a complete family. He studied his sister for a moment before he looked around at the footsteps approaching them.

"Berneen?" Baird's voice was low and she looked up at him. "Barnabas is here. I think we can go in now."

She turned her head, and the two men drew in a deep breath, seeing the devastation on her face, realizing just how hard it would be for her.

Barnabas looked around, spying Buckley and motioning him over.

"Buckley? Pray, please." Barnabas' words were almost curt, to cover his emotions.

Buckley's prayer sought wisdom, peace, guidance and protection for them. Berneen swiped at the tears on her face, pausing as a large white handkerchief appeared in her line of sight. She hadn't known that Baird carried one. Then she sighed. There was so much she didn't know about him and wasn't sure if she ever would.

Baird's hand gripped hers tight as she walked up the steps to the wide covered porch and then squeezed harder as she hesitated at the door, her own hand reaching for Darby.

"Darby, do you remember anything?"

He nodded. "I remember us playing on the porch. I don't know that anything has changed here." He walked through the door, curiosity on his face as he studied the hallway and then walked through the rooms.

Berneen stood in the hallway, staring around, then looking up the oak stairway to the second floor, before she too moved through the lower floor, stopping every once in a while as memories stirred in her mind, reaching for objects, books, pictures. She finally stood in the room that had been her father's office, one arm around her waist, the other hand on her face, as her head moved. She fought back the tears. She knew Barnabas and the men were around, she could hear quiet footsteps and low conversation. She also knew that there were still police officers around. The chief had come to her, stating that her father had been a good friend of his, and he was sorry for how it had all been handled. She had been gone before he knew what was happening. They were searching, he said, for proof of what she had just reported.

She moved away from the office, heading for the stairs, finding Darby standing staring into the room that had been their parents. She stood with him, arms around one another.

"Has anything changed, Neen?"

She shook her head. "It's exactly as we left it that night. I mean, cleaners have been through but I don't see anything missing." She moved forward, towards the dresser. "Mom had a secret compartment she kept her jewelry in. Let me see if it's still there." She reached behind the mirror, feeling for a moment, before a section of wall moved and a shallow closet appeared.

Darby stared at it and then at Berneen, watching as she moved towards the closet, her hands reaching for the drawers and pulling them open.

Baird stood in the doorway, not sure what she had just done, watching as she came back out, laying what she had in her hands on the dresser.

"Berneen?" Darby's voice questioned her.

"Just a sec, Darb." She looked through the jewelry cases and boxes and then re-entered the closet. She breathed a sigh of relief as she came back out. "It's all here. Nothing is missing,"

"Berneen? Will you take that with you?" Baird walked towards her. "I know the guys brought boxes with them in case there were things you wanted to take with you."

She looked up at him, relief on her face. "There are some things, if you have room for them in your apartment."

"Ours." She frowned at him. "It's our apartment, Berneen. Not mine anymore. And yes, we have room for whatever you want to take."

She nodded. "Okay, then. What's here on the dresser." She looked around. "I think that's all for this room." She walked away, stopping in the doorway of her own bedroom, tears suddenly blinding her.

Darby reached for his sister, the siblings clinging together, before she moved forward, looking around. "Just the photos in here, I think, Baird." She reached for one, his hand stopping her.

"The guys will pack what you want. Just tell them." He looked back at Barnabas, who nodded.

"Oh. Okay, then." She moved away, not seeing the look on his face as she did so. "Darby? I'm not sure what to take from your room."

Darby stared around, not really remembering anything. It was a child's room, he thought, and then sighed. That's what he had been when he had been forced to leave. He picked up a stuffed bear, memories coming with it.

"This, Neen. I want this."

She nodded, her hand touching it lightly. "They gave that to you just as they were leaving. Mom said it was full of hugs and kisses, enough to do until they came back."

He nodded soberly. "I remember. I felt so lost when I knew we didn't have it with us."

"We didn't have time to plan. Small made us leave so quickly."

Chapter 26

Baird watched Berneen closely as she moved through the main floor of the house, indicating what she wanted to take with her, worried at her silence and withdrawal. Buckley stood beside him, concern colouring his face.

"Are you okay, Baird?"

Baird shrugged. "It's hard, Buckley. I see them doing this, coming back to their home after so many years, having to fight their grief once more. I never really got to do that. The house was destroyed so soon after Dad went home."

"She's trusting you and she's trusting us, whether she realizes it or not."

Baird nodded. "I see that. It will take time for her to do that fully though, if she ever does." He paused, not quite sure how to proceed. "How do we go on, Buckley? How do we get through the next few weeks? Coming back here will open up a wealth of emotions she has just buried, both for herself and for Darby. She's grieving for both of them."

"I know, Baird. I've put a call into a friend, asking if she would talk with her." Buckley stared at Berneen as she stood at her father's desk before she sank into his chair, her hand rubbing along the polished wood. "Baird, do you have room for the desk?"

Baird stared at him, uncertain as to the change of topic. "I can do. In the den. Why?"

"Because she needs it. She needs that contact with her father. Darby muttered something about his mother giving the desk to their father."

"Okay." Baird looked around, stopping as Buckley's hand came to rest on his shoulder.

"We'll look after it. Find out if there is anything else in furniture she wants. We can put it in one of the storage units for now."

"Thanks, Buckley." Baird moved towards Berneen, crouching down beside her, an arm around her. "You okay?"

She nodded, slowly. "I think so. There have been so many memories, I'm overwhelmed. I need to pack his desk and the filing cabinets. Do we have room for boxes, Baird?"

"We do. I have a storage unit that we can put things in when you've sorted through them." He looked around. "Didn't you say your father had a safe?"

"He did." She shoved back the chair, rising, and walking towards the entry, pausing at a certain point, her hands feeling along the chair rail moulding, before Baird heard a click and a section of the wall popped open.

"What is it with these?" He was trying to lighten the mood for her.

She gave a half smile. "Dad liked mysteries and puzzles. He did these two. I think there is another one but I don't remember for sure." She punched in the digital code and then turned the handle on the safe, pulling it open. She stared at what was inside, her breath in her throat. "I think we'll just clear it all out, Baird, and take it with us."

"That sounds like a plan."

Berneen took one last walk through the house, her arms wrapped around herself. She knew Darby had done that and then gone out to explore the yard and outbuildings, some of Baird's friends with him. Baird waited patiently for her, one shoulder against the arched doorway to the living room. His thoughts were bleak, wondering how she would leave this to live in his apartment. He sighed to himself, knowing that he had never planned to move from there. It was his home, his sanctuary, but now he knew he had to face giving it up, moving from there, away from the men he considered his family. He just wasn't sure he could do that.

"Berneen?" She had stopped in front of him, not looking at him, her eyes on the floor, her arms wrapped around herself. "We have time. We don't have to leave yet."

"No, it's okay. I'm ready to go." She looked up, her emotions hidden. "I needed this, Baird. It's not home anymore. Not with Mom and Dad gone. It's Darby's if he wants it. If he doesn't, then I don't know what I'll do."

"You mean that, don't you?" At her nod, he just swept her into a hug, a kiss dropped on her head. "Don't make any rushed choices. We'll keep it and over time, we can discuss it and decide from there." He turned her to face the front door. "Just know that no matter what you decide, I back you every step of the way."

She looked up at him, wonder in her eyes. "You mean that, Baird?"

"I do. You're my wife. I can't do anything else but that." He looked down at her, tumult in his heart as the ice melted more and more and he admitted to himself finally that he was beginning to care deeply for the lady he held right at that time.

Sudden yells from outside the house had Baird shoving Berneen down and covering her with his body despite her struggles to get up. He could hear distinct popping sounds as well as shouts to put down the weapon. An officer was beside them suddenly, a hand on Baird's back keeping them down.

"Darby! Baird! Where's Darby?" Berneen struggled to free herself, unable to as Baird's weight kept her on the floor. "Baird? Get off me. I need to find Darby."

There was sudden silence outside, then more calls, this time for paramedics. Baird knew Brady would in the thick of it. He sat up, his arms still around Berneen, the officer's hand still on his shoulder.

"Baird, let me go. I need to find Darby." Berneen's anger flared as she shoved at him.

"No, we wait, Berneen. We have to wait. They'll let us know when we can leave here." His arms tightened on her even as his heart raised in prayer. Please, Lord, not Darby. Don't take him from her.

A few minutes, Baird looked up as quiet footsteps approached, and Barnabas and Buckley stood for a moment, worry, concern, and another emotion he couldn't place.

"Barnabas? Buckley?"

His voice raised Berneen's head and she stared at the men before she shoved away from him, on her feet, running for the outside door, slipping on the polished hardwood, and then she was outside, her voice calling for Darby.

"I'm sorry, Baird. He was hit. How bad, we're not sure. Small took us by surprise, coming in from the back of the lot. Brady's with him." Barnabas' voice held sorrow and concern, knowing how this would affect Baird's Berneen.

Baird scrambled to his feet, his only thought finding Berneen.

Chapter 27

Berneen struggled to reach her brother, held back by some of Barnabas' men, her eyes wide in shock and horror as she watched them work over him, Brady right there in the thick of the paramedics. She couldn't tell how bad it was, but she knew he was unconscious. She watched as they finally lifted him to a stretcher, and then ran with the stretcher towards the waiting paramedic rig, his coat and shirt cut away, blood covering his arm, a large bandage wrapped around it, oxygen mask in place, IV line running to his hand. Berneen tried to follow but found herself held in Baird's arms.

"We'll follow, Berneen. Come on. Brody has a car for us. They'll give us an escort there." He shoved her into the waiting vehicle, his eyes on her, following her to a seat and slamming the door behind him..

He pulled her from the vehicle as Brody stopped at the Emergency entrance and ran with her inside, stopping at the clerk's desk.

"Darby Dakin was just brought in. This is his sister. She's his next of kin for medical purposes."

The clerk looked up and then nodded to some chairs. "Wait there. I'll let them know you're here."

Berneen huddled against Baird, her eyes not moving from the door, not sure if Darby was even alive. She had noise around her but didn't stir. She felt a hand on her arm and finally looked around, seeing Barnabas there.

"Barnabas? What happened?"

"Small snuck up on us all. He had been under surveillance and somehow managed to slip away." He looked down for a moment, swallowing hard. "I'm sorry, Berneen. We thought we had you two safe."

"You did, I think. You did what you had to."

"I know, but it wasn't enough. Darby shouldn't have been hurt. We had men with him and he was still got to." Barnabas bit back the anger he was feeling. This had never happened to him before, and he didn't like it, not one bit.

She looked up as she heard footsteps heading her way and was on her feet, moving the meet the physician before Baird could stop her. He was right after her, his arm around her.

"Doctor? How is Darby?"

"A lucky young man. It looked a lot worse than it was. The bullet winged his arm, but didn't break anything. A few stitches and he'll be good to go. He informed me that he was not staying in here."

"No, he won't. Doc will look after him, as will Brady. And I'm sure Anna will smother him with care." Baird spoke up at that point.

The physician peered at Baird. "Baird? You here?"

"I am, Bill. This is my wife, Berneen, and that's her brother, Darby."

———

"Married? I hadn't heard, Baird." Bill studied his friend and then Berneen. "Congratulations. I didn't know you had been dating."

"Long story, Bill, for another day. Can we see Darby?"

"In a few minutes. The nurse is just keeping him cleaned up. He's not a happy camper."

Berneen laughed, tears not far off. "He never is when he's sick. I should know. I've nursed him on my own for the last ten years." She moved away from the two men, intent on finding Darby.

"What did she just say?" Bill spun to watch her.

"She's raised him since he was five and she was eighteen. Their parents were killed overseas, and there was no one else. Again, another long story."

"You and your long stories. We need to do coffee soon." Bill walked away, his hand already reaching for the chart the charge nurse was holding out to him.

"Baird? How's Darby?" Barnabas stood beside him.

As Baird turned, he saw the rest of the men standing behind them, stern looks on their faces.

"Just a graze, I think he said. Nothing serious. He'll be ready to go home soon." He looked around to where Berneen stood, her eyes on her brother. "This is not going to help, guys. Not at all."

"No, it won't. And it won't help when she hears Small is dead. He didn't give the officers any choice." Brody stood next to Baird. "Who gets to tell her that?"

"I guess I do."

Barnabas shook his head at Baird's words. "No, the chief will come and talk to her later tonight. He wants to tell her himself."

Chapter 28

Her head cushioned on her folded arms, Berneen rested at the kitchen table later that evening. Baird had set a cup of her peppermint tea in front of her, rested his hand on her back, and then walked away, his mug of coffee in his hand. He was making room for her things, he said. She just shook her head, not even able to think about that. She thought back over the afternoon, a frown on her face. There had been something off in her father's office and she didn't know what. She jumped to her feet and then caught herself as her head spun.

She ran for Baird, finding him standing staring at her father's desk, looking around as she ran into the room.

"Baird? Can someone take pictures or a video of my Dad's office?"

He shrugged. "We can. Why?"

"Something was different. I don't know what. Maybe if I have pictures, I can tell."

Baird nodded, made a quick phone call and then reached to pull her into a hug. "Benen will look after that. He still has the keys. He said he'd head over there now."

"Now? Baird, it's too late."

Baird shook his head. "He wants to. He'll bring copies by tomorrow." He turned her in his arms, making her face the room. "Your Dad's desk fits just right."

"It does. Thank you, Baird. I thought it would be too crowded." Her heart was hurting for her brother, but she knew it was opening up to Baird. He was wiggling his way in without even trying. She sighed to herself, knowing she was beginning to care deeply for him, if not love him, and that scared her.

"The police chief wanted to come by tonight, but I put him off." Baird's quiet voice broke into her thoughts.

"Small's dead. What more can he say?"

"How'd you know?"

She shrugged. "I just did."

His chin on her head, he waited, knowing that she would speak when she was ready. If not tonight, then maybe tomorrow.

"I don't know how well Dad knew him. That's the thing. How did he get involved in our lives? What was he after?" Berneen moved away from Baird, leaving him to sit back against his desk, arms folded across his chest. "How do we find out?"

"We'll find out. The police are investigating now, the chief has said that. Barnabas won't rest until he finds out why and how."

"It's too dangerous. Today proved that." Berneen walked away, leaving Baird to drop his head in frustration before he was out of the room and after her.

"Neen? Take the bed tonight? No arguments?"

She glared at him before she gave an abrupt nod, heading for the bedroom, stopping first in Darby's doorway to watch him, a prayer rising for healing for her baby brother.

Baird watched her disappear and then walked to the front door as he heard a quiet tap at it, opening it to find Breck standing there. He stepped back, Breck walking through the doorway, hesitation in his manner.

"Breck?" Baird was puzzled at his friend stopping by that late.

"Baird, go. Get some sleep. I'll watch for Darby." Breck watched as Baird's eyes slid closed before he nodded and walked away.

God, I have no idea where we're going with this. Protect these three. It was too close today for Darby. Breck headed for the kitchen, knowing it was going to be a long night, and he would need coffee to keep him awake.

Baird hesitated for a moment before he pulled a blanket from the closet and then laid down on top of the bedspread, covering himself with the blanket, his arms reaching for Berneen, pulling her close to him, his head against hers as he drifted off to sleep, trying to pray, but unable to form any words, confident in his heart that God knew what he wanted and needed to say.

Chapter 29

Berneen scowled at the photos spread out in front of her the next morning, not sure what she was seeing or if she could even trust her memory any more. She closed her eyes to envision, if she could, what the office had looked like. A sudden thought had her eyes open and her hands scrambling through the photos, stilling as she found the one she wanted. She stared at it, and then was on her feet, running through the apartment. Breck looked askance at her.

"Baird? Where is he?"

"I think in his office." Breck was on his feet. "Why?"

"Because I found out what is wrong in Dad's office." She spun, heading for the door. "Does he have clients, do you know?'

Breck shrugged. "I'm not sure. He might have." He was torn, wanting to go with her, but needing to stay with Darby, who had been up and then gone back to sleep. "Berneen! Wait. Let me get someone to go down with you."

She spun. "I'm only going to the first floor. Is that an issue?"

Breck's hand drew her back from the door. "It might be. We have security, but someone could conceivably get in. We need to take steps to make sure you're safe even here."

She paled, not realizing that she could be in danger in the Foundation building. "Here? Breck?" She turned as she heard a knock at the door.

Breck opened it slowly to find Anna standing there, crock pot in hand, a smile on her face.

"Good morning, Breck. Just bringing in a meal for all of you." She walked past him, deposited the pot on the counter, plugging it in, and then turned to sweep Berneen into a tight hug. "Now, your brother? Is he up?"

"Darby was up earlier, before Berneen was. He's sleeping again." Breck reached for Berneen's arm. "Now that Anna's here, we can go find Baird."

Berneen hesitated at the door to Baird's office, as she watched him deep in his work, not willing to disturb him. She clutched the photo in her hand, knowing that when she spoke, it would change things for her. It would change a memory that she had of her father.

Breck had no trouble disturbing Baird, showing he had done that very thing many times before.

"Baird. Can you mark your place and take a moment?"

Baird's finger went up as he ignored Breck. Fifteen minutes later, he sat back, his eyes on his drawings before he nodded and then looked around, coming to his feet and approaching Berneen as she stood, hesitating, ready to turn and flee.

"Berneen. I didn't know you were here. You need to speak up, Sweetheart. I would have stopped where I was if I had known."

She stared at him before she snapped her mouth closed. She wasn't used to that, she thought. "It's okay. You needed to finish that. You just thought Breck was here."

"No, it's not okay. You have a voice. You need to use it to let me know where you are and what you want and how you feel." He wrapped her in a hug, a frown on his face as he looked at Breck.

Breck just shook his head. Lord, you need to work with these two. They're in love with one another, afraid to speak about it, afraid to trust one another. Bring that trust to them. Help them to trust You more and more each day.

"Berneen has a photo, I think, in her hand that she needs to talk to you about." Breck turned, hand on the doorknob, when Berneen's hand gripped his arm and pulled him back.

"No, please, Breck. You need to stay. Maybe you'll see something I have missed." She slipped from Baird's arm and slapped the photo on his desk. "This. This is what has me puzzled."

Baird studied it, then shook his head, his gaze on Breck, who stood beside him, studying first the photo and then Berneen.

"Berneen? What is it you see that you don't like?" Breck spoke finally, when Berneen had just stood there, staring at Baird, a puzzled look on her face.

"I'm sorry. What did you ask, Breck?" Berneen finally looked at him, and then at the photo.

"Talk to us. Tell us what that area should look like and what you see that makes it different."

Baird reached for a white china marker. "Here. Use this. We can get other copies of the photo. Do you need it enlarged?"

Berneen stared at him, her thoughts muddled, before Breck sighed, reached for the photo and headed for Baird's copier, enlarging the photo and bringing it back, placing it in front of her. He reached for her hand that held the marker and set it against the photo.

"Berneen? If you can? Can you mark what's different?"

"I guess." She shrugged as she moved to stare down at the photo. Her thoughts traced back to playing in that office with her father working away, looking up every once in a while to interact with her. She thought of being in there the night before her parents flew out, somehow knowing that trip would change their lives, but never imaging how much it would.

Her fingers traced through the photo, her mind working, before she began to mark what she knew and what she thought was different.

"There. I think that's it. Those pictures. The knick-knacks. Dad hated things like that in his office. He said it was distracting to have odds and sods sitting around, as he put it. Those books. They're not his. He disliked that author."

She looked up. "Can we go back there, Baird? I didn't pack those things. I need to see them in real life."

He glanced at his watch, made a quick calculation, and then nodded. "Just let me make a quick phone call. I'm not quite where I should be with the plans. Not your fault!" His hand went up as she opened her mouth to protest and then clamped it shut. "They knew it might take a bit of time. I'm sourcing materials right now for them, not what I usually do, but they asked. I have to wait for some replies."

Chapter 30

Berneen watched as Baird unlocked the door to her childhood home, not sure she wanted to be there again, but knowing she had to. She would likely have to come back again and again, just to dispel the sadness she felt, but she wasn't even sure that would work. She prayed for peace, for the burden to be lifted, and felt a lightening of her burden.

Breck and Benen stood behind her, their backs to them, watchful. They knew Small had not been working alone. What they were not sure of was how much the other person or people were involved with this house.

Baird opened the door, stepping through, his hand reaching for hers, waiting as she hesitated in the hallway, a frown on her face, before she walked through to the office. She reached for the box he carried but he shook his head, setting it on a small table, and then reaching to hug her. She could hear his softly-uttered prayer and then stepped away from him, her eyes on the photos as she gathered them and held them out to him, working quickly to gather everything she had noted different.

Benen finally spoke. "Is there anything else that seems off here, Berneen?"

She looked at him in surprise, not having thought of that, just wanting to get in and out. "I don't think so. Let me walk around here and I'll see." She walked the office, hesitating every once in a while to indicate something off and that object was gathered up into boxes as well.

The three men watched as she walked the whole house, finding objects she said were not theirs, had not been there before, and they gathered each one for her.

Finally, she stood on the back porch, looking around the yard. "I just don't know, Baird. Everything has grown so much in the last ten years. I can't tell if things are different."

"That's okay, Sweetheart. We'll work with what you've taken." He turned as Breck approached from around the house. "Do you want anything more from here today?"

She shook her head, walking down the steps and along the flagstone path to the front yard.

Baird stared after her before he spoke. "I don't think she'll want to come back here."

"No, I don't think she will. Darby will, but he doesn't have the memories that she does." Breck walked beside Baird as they followed Berneen. "What happens to the house?"

"It stays as it is until Darby is 18. I mean, they can live in it, or rent it, but Berneen said they can't sell it. I'm not sure, but I think she said it can't ever be sold."

"Wow! That's something. It's a nice house, has good bones as you would say."

"It is. But I don't think she'll want to live in it. And I'm not sure if she could even come visit Darby here. There's been too much taken away from it and her."

"I can see that." Breck stood and watched as Baird approached Berneen, moving her to the vehicle and into it, before he too stood, his eyes on the house before they dropped to Breck and he shook his head.

Breck sighed, knowing that whatever these two were going through, it was not over, not by a long shot, he thought. He approached the car, his eyes catching the forlorn look on Berneen's face before her gaze met his and then flickered away quickly, but not so quickly that he didn't see the sheen of tears in her eyes.

Baird stood later that afternoon, back from his office in the lower floors, and watched Darby. He was standing in the office doorway, his eyes on his sister, wanting to go to her but making no move to do so, not sure how to approach her as she worked through the material she had brought back with her.

Baird stopped beside Darby, an arm around his shoulder for a moment, before he nodded towards the kitchen.

"Has she eaten at all?" He kept his voice low.

Darby shook his head, and Baird could see the worry in his eyes. "No. I can't get her to leave that stuff. She won't talk to me, won't leave it, has stayed in there since she came back."

"Leave it to me. How's the arm?" Baird grinned at the grimace Darby made. "Like that, huh? How be you do what you can to find us a meal? I'll deal with Neen."

"Baird, why do you call her Neen? That's what we've always done. I guess that's my fault. I couldn't say her full name, just Neen, and it stuck."

Baird shrugged, not sure himself why he did. "I have no idea. It just suits her."

Baird stood for a moment, his eyes on Berneen, before he moved behind her, his arms coming around her and stilling her movements. "Have you taken a break since we got back?"

She shook her head. "I wanted to keep working at this. There's something here. I'm just not seeing it."

"You need to step back and take a break. I found Darby in the doorway, wanting to talk to you, but not wanting to interrupt you."

"That's crazy. He could have." She could feel anger starting to build in her, not directed at Baird or Darby.

"He didn't know, Berneen. He thinks he can't." Baird just stood, his arms dropping to his side. "You two need to talk, Berneen. He's hurting, not just physically. He's been back to a house he really doesn't remember. He sees you're hurting and upset but won't talk to him."

She spun. "Don't tell me how my brother is. I think I know."

"Berneen, you know him, but this is something neither one of you have faced before. You need to communicate with him."

She shoved at him, not able to move him. "Baird, I know him. He would talk to me. He always has."

"Berneen, listen to me. You're married now. In his eyes, that changes things. He knows your relationship has changed all of a sudden. He's been thrown into a new home, been hurt, sees his sister shutting him out."

They continued to argue back and forth, neither giving way, until Baird sighed, swept her into his arms and kissed her, silencing the hurt angry words she was about to speak. He raised his head, his eyes on her, watching as she stared up at him and then opened her mouth to argue once more. His face dropped to hers as he kissed her again.

Darby slid back into his chair in the kitchen. He had opened the door to Blair, who entered and headed for the coffee pot, his head tilting as he heard the voices in the office.

"They're arguing? Baird never argues."

Darby grinned. "She's trying. He's not." He looked around as the voices went silent and his grin grew bigger.

Blair stared at him. "You think this is funny?"

Darby shook his head. "I do. Berneen is trying her best to argue but Baird isn't."

Blair stared at him for a moment before he too grinned. "I see. It's like that is it?"

"What's the saying? Kiss and make up?" Darby began to laugh as Blair just shook his head. "I would say Berneen is doing the fighting, Baird's doing the making up part."

Berneen leaned against Baird, her head to his chest, hearing the strong steady beat of his heart, knowing that he cherished her. But did he love her? That was what she was not yet sure of. If she could be, then maybe life would be different. But would she walk away from him, taking Darby with her? Would Darby even go?

Baird regretted his hastiness at kissing Berneen, without asking her if he could. But she looked so cute, he thought, standing up to him, her hair loose around her shoulders for once. He figured that whatever was left of his heart for her to steal would be considered stolen. He wanted to spend the rest of his life with her, God willing, but he didn't know if that was how she felt.

Chapter 31

The next morning, Baird stood where Berneen had stood, seeing what she had seen, and he felt the fear running through him once more that he had felt when Darby was hurt. The people after Berneen were vicious, he could see that. He wasn't sure if she had picked up on what he was seeing. His phone in his hand, he hesitated, staring at it, not sure who to call. He turned as he heard footsteps on the floor behind him. Barnabas walked towards him with a man he didn't know.

"Baird? This is John Paul. He's a friend, an investigator, that I spoke with. I didn't say anything to you or Berneen as I wasn't sure he would be free. He informs me he freed up his schedule just to work on this."

Baird reached to shake the older man's hand, noting the graying hair and the lines of life on the man's face. "Thank you. Now, what do you need to know?"

"I need to talk to you, to your wife, and her brother. Are they available?"

"I think so. Berneen was still sleeping a few minutes ago. Darby had been up and was heading to see Doc." Baird moved to reach for his phone sitting on his desk.

Barnabas' hand stopped his moving away. "Let me call Doc. He'll bring him back. You wake Berneen."

"I'm behind you, Barnabas. Did you grab yourself a coffee on the way by?" Berneen moved past the two men, handing Baird his mug of coffee, positioning herself so she was tight to his side, his arm coming around her, as she sipped at her tea.

"No, we didn't but we can. John?"

"Sounds good, Barnabas." John studied the younger couple in front of him. "Berneen? May I call you that?" At her nod, he set the folders he had been carrying down on Baird's desk. "Thank you. I worked with your father a few times. I am sorry for your loss."

She tilted her head, a frown on her face. "You did? And thank you." She wasn't quite sure of the man standing in front of them, not quite liking what she was reading from him. "I don't remember Dad speaking of you at all."

John shook his head. "He wouldn't have as it was work related." He looked around. "Barnabas has done a nice job on these apartments."

Neither one of the couple responded, leaving John to move restlessly, before Barnabas was back, handing him a mug of coffee.

"So, Berneen? What have you found?" Barnabas watched her closely, seeing the shuttered look that came over her face. What is wrong, Lord? Who doesn't she trust? His eyes shifted to Baird, watching as the other man studied John, a frown on his face.

Barnabas sighed to himself, not sure if he had done the right thing after all. He motioned to Baird, who moved towards him, and then followed Barnabas into the hallway.

"Barnabas?"

"I'm sorry, Baird. I should have asked you first." Barnabas took a sip of his coffee, watching Berneen, who had shuffled the photos into a pile and then into a folder before she moved away from John, setting the folder on Baird's desk. She then moved around the desk to sit in his chair, her eyes on John.

"No problem, Barnabas. I just don't get Berneen's reaction. She's reading something about him that I'm not."

"She is." Barnabas paused, his eyes on John. "You know, he just doesn't sound like the John I knew." He walked away, his phone out, heading for privacy to make a call.

Baird moved back towards Berneen, perching on the side of the desk, his hand on hers where they rested on the desktop.

"So, John, tell me. What all have you worked on for Barnabas?"

John looked at him, shaking his head. "Can't tell you that. All my investigations are kept confidential." He leaned back against a table, setting his mug down, and folding his arms. "I feel like you two don't trust me."

160

"Why should we?" Berneen's words had a bite to them. "We don't know you. Have never seen you. I doubt very much if what you have in those folders will help at all."

"And why would you say that? You have no idea what I have."

Berneen shook her head, her eyes narrowing. "I just have a feeling, Mr. Paul. And I have learned to go with my gut instincts. That says you are not who you are saying you are."

John Paul laughed. "Your gut instincts? Really?" He looked with amusement at her before he spoke again. "Is that how your wife goes through life, Baird?"

Baird's face tightened as he too became suspicious of the man in front of them. "I trust her instincts. I doubt she is saying what she is without knowing something." He looked down at Berneen, a question of his face for a moment, before he nodded. He stood, tall and strong, Berneen thought, ready to face anything that was thrown at him. She trusted him with her life and now her heart. He would do his best to protect her.

John Paul shook his head. "You two have no idea what you're talking about."

Baird's attention was caught for a second by a whisper of sound from the kitchen area, not sure what was going on. He heard a muted sound from Berneen and looked back at John Paul, seeing him standing now in front of him, a wicked looking knife in his hand.

"Whoa!" Baird backed away, standing in front of Berneen. "Wait a minute! What's going on here?"

"Your wife is what's going on here. She needs to come with me." The older man moved towards them, Baird shoving Berneen away from him.

"Run, Berneen. Get out of here." Baird felt the angry slash of the knife in his abdomen, a shocked, disbelieving look covering his face even as his hands reached for the area, one hand coming back as he stared down at it in horror, before his legs crumpled and his body slumped to the floor, not moving. The older man stood over him, reaching down to wipe the blood from the knife on Baird's shirt before he walked over, picked up his folders and his mug and then left.

Berneen hesitated before she ran for the doorway, sliding to a stop as she saw the man standing there, his hands reaching to grasp her arms, a hand coming around her mouth as he grappled with her. She fought him, desperate to escape, to fight help for Baird and Barnabas. Where was Barnabas, she thought? A sharp prick in her arm sent her mind whirling as darkness swirled around her and she slumped, gathered quickly into the man's arm and carried from the apartment, down the back stairs and then dumped into a waiting vehicle. She didn't see John Paul slide into the front seat, his head turned for a moment as he watched her closely before he nodded and the vehicle sped away, out of the back driveway and away from the building where she had felt safe.

Chapter 32

Doc tapped at the door of the apartment, frowning when he had no answer. His hand stopped Darby from walking in.

"Wait, Darby. I don't like this." He spun the young man around and headed for the next apartment. "Stay in here."

Doc walked back to Baird's apartment door, hesitating for a moment. He heard footsteps approaching and turned to see Branigan and Bradon approaching.

"Doc? What's going on?" Branigan stopped, his eyes worried. "We got a call from Barnabas that he needed us here."

"That's what I was afraid of. I've stuck Darby away in Benen's apartment for now." He reached for the doorknob, before Branigan's hand stopped him.

"Let us go first, Doc." He cautiously opened the door, not speaking, Benen right behind him.

They stopped, frozen in time for a moment, as they spied Barnabas' body, sprawled facedown on the kitchen floor, not moving, a large wound on the side of his head, the blood not congealed as yet. Benen stooped, feeling for a pulse, and nodding, before he pointed to the rest of the apartment.

The two men searched quickly and then when they reached the office, gave a cry of alarm and sprang forward to where Baird lay, hands assessing him.

"Go get Doc, Benen. See if Brady's around too."

"He's on duty. I'll put in the call." Benen's phone was in his hand even as he moved quickly to find Doc and point towards the office. "In there, Doc. Baird's hurt bad. I'll stay with Barnabas."

Doc shot him a quick look before he too bent over Barnabas. "That's a nasty blow. I'll be back as soon as I can." He almost ran for the study, seeing the look of distress on Benen's face.

He paused for a moment, finding Branigan with his hands pushing a towel against Baird's abdomen. Branigan had shifted Baird carefully to his back and then ran for towels to try and stop the bleeding.

"How long?" Doc was on his knees, his hands moving the towel, looking around for scissors. "Scissors?"

Branigan searched, finding a pair in a desk drawer, and handing them to Doc.

"I don't think that long, Doc. Barnabas called me not five minutes ago." He looked around. "Where's Berneen?"

"She's not here? Look for her, boy." Doc's attention was directed at assessing the wound, frustrated that he didn't have the supplies he needed. "Where are the paramedics?"

"Benen called." Branigan searched the apartment, standing aside as the paramedics rushed in, followed by the police officers. He frowned. She was nowhere to be seen. He looked up as he heard a sound at the door and saw Darby standing in the entrance, fear, no terror, Branigan thought, on his face and moved towards him, not realizing how much blood he had on his hands or shirt.

"Darby?"

"Branigan! You're bloody! Where's Berneen? Where's Baird?" Darby's voice was rising in his panic even as Branigan moved him backwards.

"I need to clean up. Back to Benen's." He waited, Darby not moving. "Darby!" Branigan's voice was sharp and lashing, not his normal voice, causing Darby to jump. "Move! Back to Benen!"

Branigan scrubbed at his hands and then looked down at his shirt, pulling it from him and ditching it into a trash can. He quickly reached in Benen's closet, pulling out a sweatshirt, knowing Benen would tell him to do just that.

He turned and watched Darby, who stood, eyes frozen on the door, not moving, before he walked over to him, an arm around the youth's shoulder.

"I don't know where your sister is. She's not there. Barnabas is down with a head wound. It looks as if he was struck from the side."

"Baird?" Darby's voice was barely audible. "Where's Baird?"

"He's hurt, Darby, hurt bad. He was stabbed. Doc's working on him as are the paramedics." He paused as he heard a tap at the door, and shoving Darby behind him, reached to open it.

He walked out to speak with the police officer, standing so he could watch Darby. He nodded before he motioned for Darby to come with him.

"We'll head to the hospital, Darby. They've taken them in."

"Is Baird alive?" Darby could barely get the words out.

"He is. I'm not sure how serious it is. I wasn't told." An arm around Darby's shoulder provided support to the youth, who stumbled as he walked.

"Berneen?"

"I'm sorry, Darby. She's not there. They don't know where she is."

Darby's heart sank, as worry for his sister filled his mind and heart. "Then, where is she?"

"We don't know. She was there when you left, right?"

Darby nodded. "She was still sleeping, I think, or just waking up. I wasn't gone that long, was I?"

"No, I don't think you were. These people move fast, that's the problem. They see an opportunity and take advantage of it." He pulled to a stop in a parking spot outside the hospital, and reached to grab Darby's arm as the youth opened the door. "We need to pray, Darby. This is testing your faith and your trust in God. Don't let it move you away from Him."

Darby stared at him, wondering how he knew just what he was feeling, before he nodded and bowed his head.

Chapter 33

Darby paced the waiting room, his eyes on the door the examination room. He needed to see Baird, needed that desperately and so far hadn't been allowed back. Brady had come through, wheeling a stretcher in, and when he was done, had stopped by him.

"Darby?"

"Brady? How's Baird?"

"Baird?" Brady spun, his eyes on the door as well. "What do you mean? How's Baird?"

"You didn't know? He was stabbed, Branigan said. They have him back there. Barnabas was hurt as well." His voice faltered for a moment. "Berneen's gone. We don't know where she is."

"Berneen?" Brady's eyes met Breck, who stood beside him, a grim look on his face. "Breck?"

"We don't know much yet. We need to talk to both Barnabas and Baird, and that's not possible, not right at the moment. The police will want their statements first before we can talk to them." He nodded at Darby. "We need him to see Baird."

Brady nodded. "Let me see what I can do." He walked away, his hand rubbing at his face, before he stopped, turned to watch Darby and then disappeared through the doors.

Ten minutes later, he was back, his hand reaching for Darby's arm. "I have permission for you to see Baird, but only for a couple of minutes. They're getting him ready to go to surgery."

"Surgery? He's hurt that bad?" Darby's voice died away. "Brady?"

"He was stabbed, Darby. Didn't you know that?" When Darby shook his head, Brady spoke once again. "He was stabbed in the abdomen. They need to take him to surgery to assess and repair the damage."

Brady watched as Darby slowly approached the stretcher Baird lay on. Darby gripped the railing, his eyes on his brother-in-law, not sure if he should speak or not. He didn't see Baird's hand raise slowly and jumped when it touched his.

"I'll be okay, Darb. Stay with Barnabas." Baird dropped off again and Darby was forced to move way as the attendants moved the stretcher out of the room and towards the elevator.

Brady pulled Darby with him. "Come on. Up to the surgical waiting room. I hear the guys are up there as is Anna." He punched the button to the elevator in an angry manner and then dropped his head. Lord, we need You right now. How we need You!

Darby sat once more, his eyes on the doors to the waiting room, watching for the surgeon to come, for a police officer to enter to say they had found Berneen. He didn't hear the muted, angry conversation around him.

———

169

"Where's Barnabas?" His question stilled the words around him.

"Barnabas was hurt too, Darby. Didn't we tell you that?" Benen spoke from where he was seated beside him.

Darby shrugged. "How bad?"

"A concussion for sure. He had a nasty cut on his head. He's still unconscious, Darby, so we can't talk to him. His secretary said he had a friend come to see him this morning and that friend and he headed to talk to your sister and Baird."

"Is he responsible?"

"We don't know. He wasn't there. There were no signs of anyone but your sister, Baird, and Berneen, other than for the condition we found the two men in." Benen's hand rested on Darby's shoulder. "We'll find her, Darby. That's a promise from all of us."

"Don't let it take so long!" Darby was angry, not at the men he considered his friends, but at the situation he found himself in.

"We'll do our best, Darby." Benen moved his head, hearing footsteps approaching the door, and the surgeon walked in, pulling off his mask and then his surgical cap before he sank into the empty chair by Darby.

"Darby? Is that correct?" The surgeon watched the youth closely as he nodded.

"That's right. How's Baird?"

"He's in recovery right now. He's a lucky man that he was found so quickly."

Darby's face whitened as he took in the words. "Doctor? What do you mean?"

"I mean with as quick of a response as he had and with Doc there right away, he'll pull through. Without that, we wouldn't be having this conversation." Compassion showed in the physician's eyes as he watched Darby's eyes close and then as he raised his gaze to take in the men sitting and standing around the youth. "I'll get you in to see him once we've moved him to the ICU."

Darby nodded, his eyes on the door, not hearing the quiet conversation around him as the physician walked away. He felt an arm around him and leaned for a moment against Anna before he rose, walking away, searching for what he had no idea. Benen followed, careful to stay back to let him have the space he needed, but eyes watchful still the same.

Chapter 34

Two days later, Baird rested back against the raised head of his bed. He had been moved to a private room, the surgeon declaring he no longer needed to be in the ICU bed. Darby paced the room, not looking at Baird, who finally sighed, his eyes raised to the ceiling as his heart raised in prayer for his young bride and for her brother, and for his friends. Barnabas had been in, seated in a wheelchair, having been told he could not walk on his own just yet. He would need to stay in the hospital for another day or so.

Baird knew Barnabas was angry and had asked for the folder of photos to be brought in to him. The men had refused, but Darby had snuck them in. That folder even now lay on his legs, unopened. Barnabas had simply handed it to him, stating he had made notes. He needed Darby to look at the photos and see if he could remember anything. He had shaken his head at the unspoken question of Baird's face. Berneen was still missing and they were no closer to finding her than they had been.

Darby finally stopped by Baird's bedside, his eyes on the folder.

"What's with the folder?"

Baird handed it to him. "Take a look. It's what your sister was working on when she disappeared. It's your Dad's office. She found some things that were off. We went back and boxed them up. I think they're likely in the storage unit."

Darby reached for the folder. "Is she alive, Baird?"

"I would think so. I doubt they have done anything to her yet." He watched as Darby's eyes slid closed and a tear trickled down his face. "Come here, Darby. I need to pray for you." His arms wrapped around the youth and he felt the hard grip Darby had on him even as Darby's body shook with sobs. "It's okay, Darby. It's okay to weep. God bottles our tears, you know. He sees your sorrow and grieves with you."

"He does?"

"He does. That's part of Who He is."

Darby finally stepped back, placing the folder on the table, and opening it, a frown on his face. "I'm not sure if I can see what she saw. I don't have the memories that she does."

"We get that, Darby. Just take a look. That's all we ask." Baird looked around him as the door squeaked open and Branigan entered, followed by Buckley.

"Okay." Lost in his thoughts, Darby studied the photos. "Do you know why she circled what she did?"

"She said that those objects and books weren't her father's. That he wouldn't have had them there."

"Oh, okay." Darby frowned. "This statue? I know it. It was in the house where I had been staying. It has the same scrapes on it." He looked up at Baird. "How did it get to our place?"

<hr>

173

"That's what we're looking at. We think Small did that, but we can't prove it."

Darby stared at him, horror suddenly on his face. "He was there. He was a friend of theirs. I met him many times." He slid his eyes closed. "He knew exactly where I was all the time."

"That changes things." Branigan's voice caused Darby to jump.

"It does, doesn't it?" Baird agreed. He shoved at the blankets. "I need out of here and now."

"Now, you don't. You're not released yet. That won't happen for a couple of days." Benen shoved him gently back. "Even with Doc and Brady on site, they won't let you go."

Baird's head went back on the pillow as his hand went to his abdomen, pain slicing through him. "You're right, Benen. But I need to be doing something."

"Work on healing. Pray. That's what you can do." Branigan reached for the folder. "Anything else, Darby?"

Darby shrugged, before he looked at Branigan. "Baird says the stuff is in the storage unit. Can I look at it?"

"That you can. You come with me now. We'll leave Benen here to make sure Baird behaves himself." He smirked at the scowl Baird sent his way.

An hour later, Darby sat back, his hands resting behind him on the floor. "I don't see anything other than that statue. Do you have the photos?"

"I do." Branigan spread them out. "How be we find what she has circled and I can take them up to my office. We'll work through them there."

Darby nodded, knowing that he didn't want to go back into Baird's apartment. Not until his sister and Baird were home. "What happens with Baird's apartment?"

"We've sent in cleaners. They've looked after getting everything back to normal." He watched Darby closely as they walked up the stairs to Branigan's office. "You're not wanting to go back there. That's a given. I'm not sure if Baird will or not. We haven't discussed that yet."

"He may not. I'm not sure Berneen will feel safe there."

"I know. We've been discussing it. Barnabas will talk to them and see what they want to do. Right now, Baird has asked for it to be painted. He needs to know the colours your sister likes."

Darby's steps slowed and then stopped, shock and surprise on his face. "He wants to know them? Why?'

"So we can repaint the apartment in the colours she feels comfortable with. He's okay with that. In fact, he asked for that before we had a chance to talk to him."

Darby's steps resumed, even as he tried to sort through his muddled thoughts. "He would do that?"

"He would, Darby. And let us know what colour you want your bedroom. He stressed that." Branigan unlocked and then shoved open his office door, depositing the box on a table in a conference room. "Here. We need to eat. Let me call in an order and then we'll get to work."

Chapter 35

Two days later, Baird moved slowly around the same table, his hand on his abdomen, Darby following him, watching closely. The man finally stopped, his hands reaching for the statue Darby had identified.

"This is the one, Darby? What is wrong with it that you two picked up on?"

Darby shrugged. "I have no idea. I know Berneen knew it didn't belong to Dad." He reached for it and in the transfer between hands, it slipped from their grasp and hit the floor, breaking into pieces. "I'm sorry, Baird. I'm so sorry. That was my fault." He was done on his knees picking up the pieces and handing them to Baird.

"It's not your fault, Darby." Baird set the pieces on the table, a frown on his face. "It looks as if it had already been in pieces and just broke along the repair lines." He picked up a piece to study it more closely. "Here, what's on this?"

Darby reached for another piece. "There's something on this as well."

Baird looked around. "Find Branigan. See if he has his camera here."

Branigan followed Darby back in, camera in hand. "Darby said you wanted this."

Baird nodded, even as he swayed on his feet. Darby shoved a chair at him and made him sit. "We dropped the statue and it broke. But I think it's been broken before. There is something on each of the pieces. I can't make them out, but if we take photos, we can enlarge them and see what we find."

"That's true." Branigan began to take pictures and then headed for the computer he had set up in the room. "Give me a moment to upload these and then we'll look at them." Even as he worked away, his eyes kept straying to Baird and then to Darby, his heart raised in prayer for the two.

He finally reached for the pages on the printer, shuffling through them as he walked back towards Baird, pausing for a moment.

"Branigan, what did you find?"

"Something interesting. I think it involves your Dad as well."

Baird's hands reached for the photos. "Why would you say that?"

"Because his name is there. On the second photo." Branigan pointed to the pile of photos Baird had dropped on the table. "It gives his name, occupation and the last building he designed. Another photo also gives your Dad's name and the last inspection he did, Darby. Somehow, your Dads are connected in a way we have determined yet."

"How is that?" Baird paused, his eyes focused on the way in front of him. "But how would that play into what's happened to Berneen?"

"That's what we have to determine and as quickly as we can. Darby? Has your sister ever said anything about your Dad's work?"

Darby shrugged. "She told me what he did, but nothing more than that." He paused. "Didn't she clear out his desk and safe? Can we look through that material?"

"We can and will." Baird was on his feet, gathering up the photos. "Branigan?"

"Right with you. Benen is here as well."

"Good. We may need to bring in all the guys. I doubt we'll keep them away." Baird moved slowly, Darby's arm linked with his to provide support.

Baird sank down in his desk chair, the photos in front of him, his eyes sliding closed for a moment before he looked up at Darby as he sorted through boxes, pulling out the ones he wanted.

"Here, Baird. I think this is it. Berneen marked them all as they were packed." He sat back for a moment. "Where do we start?"

"We start by organizing by year, I would think, or by topic." Bradon reached for some of the papers, the other men's hands there as well, Brady just coming in, still in his paramedic uniform.

"Baird?" Brady stopped beside him. "Are you sure you should be up?"

"No, I'm not. But I have to." Baird looked up at Brady. "I need to do this. I told Berneen I would back her in what she was doing. I have to do the same with

Darby." He blinked rapidly for a moment to clear his eyes. "Have you heard anything yet?"

Brady shook his head. "Nothing. And I would hear rumours of some kind on the street. It's silent."

"So where is she then?" Baird reached for the papers he was being handed. "How do we do this, Brady?"

"We start with names, dates, addresses." He looked around. "Can we put up paper somewhere, Baird?"

Baird nodded. "We can. There are some small rolls of newsprint there. Tape in the cupboard."

He watched as his friends worked through what they had found, Anna bringing in a meal, Doc finally hauling him to his feet and hand on his back, directing him to his bed.

"You need to rest, Baird." Doc examined his wound and then watched closely as Baird laid back before pulling a blanket over him. "You need to sleep and recover. Not doing that won't help Berneen."

"I know, Doc. I just want to be part of what they're doing."

"And you will be. Give yourself some time." Doc watched as Baird slept, before he turned, shaking his head as he did so. The men were all like sons to him, and he hurt when they hurt. This time, though, there was nothing in his medical bag to help heal a broken heart.

Chapter 36

Branigan looked up at a sudden sound from Buckley, and then walked towards where he was sitting.

"Buckley?"

"I think I'm figuring it out, Branigan. Look. There are the fathers' names. Their occupations. Addresses where they were involved in either construction or inspection. They overlap in ways we didn't see, did we? There are a number they don't connect on, but these five? They were involved in them." Buckley rose, searching for a clear sheet of paper and marking down the addresses. "Now, we have to determine if anything happened to these properties. Who the owners are now. Insurance. Debts. Mortgages."

They stared at Buckley for a moment before Brody shook his head.

"Are you sure you're not an investigator, Buckley?"

Buckley just grinned. "It goes with how I approach my messages. I search Scripture for connections and confirmation. I don't get up and make Scripture match what I say. I make what I say match Scripture." He pointed to the paper. "This is the same idea. We are just making the facts speak for themselves. They point to someone and something, with proof there."

―――

"And we need the proof in order to go to the authorities." Braden looked around. "Breck, are they okay with us doing this?"

Breck shrugged. "They don't know about this. They would just look it over, likely, and then give it back to us. There is nothing that we have seen that would lead conclusively to anyone or any company."

"Okay, so where does this lead us?" Branigan walked over to study the paper, his face suddenly paling. "Benen, did you see this?"

Benen stood beside him in an instant, his face paling as well. "Isn't that the client Baird was working with that suddenly withdrew their plans? He had a bad feeling he said all along about him."

"He did." Branigan pulled out his phone. "I need to talk to the detective. Then we need to talk to Barnabas."

"We do." Benen was out of the door, heading for Barnabas, stopping as he met him in the hallway. "Barnabas?"

"Benen. I take it you are all in there?" He pointed towards the door.

"We are. I was just coming to find you. Buckley has sorted through everything so quickly, I can't get over how he did it. He's come up with some names and details we need to talk about."

"That's good." Barnabas paused for a moment. "Baird? Darby?"

"Doc sent Baird to bed. Darby is right there in the office, in the midst of what we're doing. He's bringing a new outlook to what we searching for, asking questions to understand what we want to find, who his father was, who Baird's father was, their occupations. Things that we take for granted that he is striving to understand. He's hurting in a way I had hoped not to see him hurt."

Barnabas nodded, his mind working through who he knew that could help him. "I might have a friend who could help him. His kids went through something."

"That would help. Barnabas, are you okay?"

"Not really. I hate this. I hate that Berneen is again missing. As for me, I have a headache that won't stop but it won't stop me. I won't let it." He walked away from Benen, coming to a stop in Baird's office doorway, his eyes searching his men, seeing their hurt for their friend but also their determination to solve whatever it was they had to solve and bring Berneen back home. He trusted them with that, that whatever they needed to do, they would do.

Branigan paused on the way past him. "I'm heading over to the house. Blair's going with me."

"Take Bradon and Kade as well. Let Kade run a search before you go in. I won't be surprised that you found some hidden objects." The men shared a glance before Branigan nodded and then called for Bradon to come with him.

Barnabas moved around the room, speaking with each one, until he stopped by Darby, dropping into a chair beside him, his eyes closing for a moment. He opened them to find Darby staring at him.

"You shouldn't be here, Barnabas." Darby's words were quiet.

"I need to be, Darby. I need to be. Benen tells me you instigated this."

Darby shrugged. "Someone had to. This is how they do it in detective movies and books, inside it? They set up white boards and cover them with data."

"That they do. Are you planning on going into that line of work?"

Darby shrugged. "I have no idea. They want me to settle on something in high school, so I know whether I want to go to college, university or trade school. Right now, I'm not sure where I want to be."

Barnabas agreed with him. "Take your time. You have your whole life ahead of you. I have friends in all trades and professions. You can talk to them, perhaps work with them for a day or so just to get a feel of what they do."

"You'd do that for me?" Darby was surprised and it showed on his face.

"Darby, it's what we do with our volunteer work. Any one of these guys would welcome you to work with them and go on their volunteer assignments if we can get approval for that."

"That's great." Darby blinked rapidly, thinking how it would have felt if his father had still be alive and able to arrange that for him. "About this?"

"Yes, this. I understand Buckley has narrowed it down."

"He has. Here are the names." Darby slid over a neatly written list. "I think I know one of them. The last name. I can vaguely remember Mom and Dad talking about him. But I can't be positive. I was so young, and it was so long ago."

Barnabas studied the youth, knowing Darby was seeking approval. "I trust you on this, Darby. If you say it's the name, we'll investigate it until we prove it otherwise. That's who we are. That's what we do."

Darby nodded, his eyes on the paper. "I think too I heard the couple I was staying with mention him. And it wasn't in a very pleasant manner. They didn't like him."

"We'll look into him." Barnabas paused. "The couple you were staying with? Did we ever get their names?"

Darby looked at him. "I have no idea if Berneen mentioned them or not." He added their names to the list. "I never did feel comfortable there but I stayed because that was where Berneen knew to reach me."

Chapter 37

The next day, Barnabas rose from behind his desk and walked through his building, stopping every once in a while from the pain of his headache. He wanted it done with but it would take time, that he knew. He rubbed at the smaller bandage Doc had put on that morning before telling him to leave the investigation to others. He had enough to do with his own work. His secretary had kept everything up to date for him, organizing the material and requests, adding her comments to them.

He stopped at Baird's office and tried the door, finding the knob turning under his hand. He entered, not surprised to find Baird there.

"Baird?"

Baird looked around, and Barnabas drew in his breath. He knew Baird had not fully recovered from his first adventure as they termed it. To see the haggard, pale face of his friend was heart-wrenching.

"Barnabas? I thought Doc had told you to stay still."

Barnabas sank into a chair. "I thought he had told you the same."

Baird sat back, his coloured pencil tapping for a moment. "He did, but I need to finish these plans. I almost had them done the other day but had to wait for some material specifications before I could. I'm sending them off shortly to the homebuyer, to see if they're what he wants."

"That's good." Barnabas just sat for a few moments. "How are you really doing, Baird?"

Baird shrugged. "Hurting. Having trouble trusting. Want Berneen back. Trying to stay strong for Darby."

"I get that. What can we do for you?"

"Find Berneen. Bring her home." Baird's voice lowered to a whisper. "I need her home, Barnabas, but I don't know if she'll be alive when she comes back."

Barnabas could hear the sorrow in his friend's voice. "We're praying that she is, Baird. I know it's likely hard to trust at this time."

"It is." Baird looked past Barnabas as the door opened and Bradon walked in.

"Bradon?"

"We have some news, Baird. Barnabas, I'm glad you're here." He pulled over a chair, his eyes on his clasped hands for a moment before he looked up. "Barnabas, your friend? John Paul? We just received word they found his body yesterday. The coroner puts his time of death as last Sunday."

"Sunday? Then, who was that who was here?" Barnabas was shaken, not sure what to think.

"He had a twin brother, who walked on the wrong side of the law. I've seen their pictures. It's hard to tell them apart."

"That's what I was picking up then. I knew something seemed off but I couldn't understand what. He had to have been the one I talked to on Monday then." Barnabas blew out a breath even as he sat back in his chair. "What did I do?"

"Someone pulled a fast one on us. Likely they didn't think you'd know until after they pulled what they did. It was a set up, Barnabas, directed at getting to Berneen." Bradon looked between the two men. "You two were incidental casualties. That's how the police have worded it. I don't think so."

Baird shook his head, even as his hands were moving to package the house drawings for courier pick up. "No, we weren't. They wanted us out of the way. They were looking to make a statement and they did. Now, what do we do with this information?"

"We look harder at him and his contacts." Barnabas drew in a deep breath. "Does the brother know the family Darby stayed with?"

"That we're looking into but it seems as if he does. The contact was Small."

"This just gets worse and worse, doesn't it?"

"It does. But does it bring us closer to finding Berneen?" Baird sat back down, his eyes on his friends. "I worry about Darby. She's all he has. I don't want to face what we've all faced, being orphans and alone." He shook his head. "Sorry, Barnabas, that didn't come out right. You're not an orphan."

"No, I'm not. But my friends are and I need to be able to understand them and how they feel. We've talked this over many times in the past." He looked around as he heard the door open and more footsteps approach. "Darby? What is it?" Barnabas was on his feet, his hand out to draw Darby closer.

Darby looked at the men, as best he could through his tears. "I got this." He held out a photo. "It's Neen. She looks as if she's dead."

Baird was on his feet, Darby wrapped in his arms as he sobbed, heartbroken at the thought his sister was dead, even as Bradon took the photo and peered at it.

"No, I don't think she is, Darby. They want her alive, why, we haven't yet figured out. They're letting us know they have her. They want to work on your emotions, Darby, Baird. We need to watch you two closely. Who's to say they won't come after one of you?"

"But why, Barnabas? What is they want?" Darby spun, fighting free to stand in front of the older man, anger radiating from him. "What do we have that they want? Or that they think we have? If Dad had been into computers and he was alive today, I would think there was a thumb drive or something that he had hidden with information on it."

Bradon's hand froze as he raised it to rub at his head, a sudden light coming to his face. "That's it. Darby, I do believe you have solved what we've been struggling with. What was in your father's office that would hide something like this?"

Darby shrugged. "I have no idea. I guess we need to go through what Berneen brought back."

"We did that. She is adamant that your father didn't place those items there." Bradon watched as Baird rose to his feet. "Baird? What are you thinking?"

"I'm thinking we need to go back to that house and if we have to pack up everything and bring it back here, we will."

"I think that is a good idea." Benen waved his phone. "I spoke with Charles. His trucks and guys are on their way there. We just need to meet them with a key." Charles was a good friend of theirs from church and owned a moving company.

"Great work." Baird was out of the office, Darby at his heels, before the other men could make a move.

Chapter 38

Baird stood in the empty house as the movers carried the last of the boxes from it, his eyes on Darby. He walked towards the youth, his hand coming to Darby's shoulder.

"Do you know of any more hiding places?"

Darby shook his head. "We talked about that. Berneen was sure there were only the two safes. The one in the bedroom. And the one in the office." He swiped a hand across his eyes before he walked up the stairs and stood in his bedroom, sorrow working through him. Please Lord? I need my Neen. Bring her home soon, Lord. I just need my sister.

Baird had followed, stopping in the doorway, his eyes on the youth and then roaming the room. He frowned and walked towards the wall opposite the door. "What's this, Darby?"

Darby looked at Baird and then the wall, finally moving to stand beside him. "What's what?"

"This? Don't you see it? The paper doesn't quite match. It was hidden behind the photo." Baird worked at the paper, removing it and then stopped, surprised at the small door he found there. Opening it, he reached in, finding a cloth sack. He felt around, finding nothing else. He felt the sack and his eyes lighted. "Come on, Darby. We hit pay dirt, I think." He moved as rapidly as he could from the room and down the stairs, Darby on his heels, even as he tucked the bag into an inside pocket of his jacket. He slid into Benen's vehicle, Darby beside him on the back seat.

"All set?" At their nod, Benen pulled from the curb, watchful but not seeing anyone that concerned him.

"They'll unload into one of the storage units, Benen?"

"They will, Baird. Blair is looking after that." He watched Baird in the mirror for a moment. "What did you find?"

"I think we found a missing piece of the puzzle. There was another hidden door in Darby's room. We would not have found it if we hadn't cleared out the house." He looked over at Darby. "We're not giving up your house, Darby. But Berneen has said she can't live in it. It's yours, she has told me. But you can't live in for three or more years."

"I don't know that I want to, Baird. Neen won't come to visit me there. I know that." Darby stared out the window, sorrow on his face, not seeing the looks the men with him were exchanging.

"We'll work it out, Darby. Don't worry about it. If we have to, it can be rented out." Baird paused. "Or it could be used for short-term stuff, like missionaries coming home on furlough and needing an address to work from."

Darby spun on the seat, the first interest in something else on his face they had seen since Berneen disappeared. "Can we do that? Or use if for people who are between homes? Like women and children?"

"That's another thought. We'll talk it over with Berneen and Barnabas."

Darby nodded. "That bag, Baird? What's in it?"

Baird pulled it out, staring at it. "I think a thumb drive." He opened the bag and shook out the contents into his hand. "I was right. A thumb drive. Thank you, Darby. You may have just solved the riddle we've been working on."

"I hope I have. We need Berneen home, safe and sound. If that does it. I hope it does." Darby turned away once more, falling silent, his eyes staring out the window again.

Baird's hand rested on Darby's shoulder before he dropped the thumb drive back into the bag and pocketed the bag.

Once in Benen's office, Baird pulled the bag out and handed it to Benen. "Can we open it, do you think?"

"I'll take a look. We may be able to." He sat down at his desk, bowed his head for a moment, and then inserted the thumb drive to his computer, running a scan on it first to ensure there were no bugs or viruses. "It's clean. Now, let's see what we can do with it."

He found he was able to open it, scanning what was coming up before he sat back, his face pale, his eyes raising to Barnabas who had followed them into his office and then to Baird and Darby. "This is bad, guys. Names, dates, addresses, information on shoddy inspections and poor designs. This is what they were after."

Barnabas pointed to the computer. "Make a copy of that. I'm taking it to the detective now." He turned as he heard Doc's voice.

"Barnabas. I just came through the lobby. Security says there's a detective to see you."

Barnabas shook his head. "No, there won't be. Benen?"

Benen tossed him the thumb drive. "Take Blair or Breck. They're driving."

Barnabas nodded and was gone before they could say another word.

Late that afternoon, Baird opened the door to his apartment to find Barnabas standing there and then stepped back so he could enter.

"Baird, you need to be in bed. You look horrible."

Baird nodded. "I will. I can relax now, I think." He walked away, a hand to his abdomen, his steps slow and hesitant.

"Doc?" Benen's voice broke the silence.

"I don't like his colour. Someone needs to check on him later tonight."

Chapter 39

Baird walked back towards his kitchen, Benen following him, late that evening. He poured their coffee, handing Benen his mug, and then stood, back to the counter, watching his friend.

Benen sat, his eyes on Baird, a frown on his face. "Have you slept, Baird?" He was concerned about the look of pain on Baird's face, the paleness, the dark circles under his eyes.

"I did for a while, then I had to get up." He sighed, his eyes dropping to his mug. "I'm trying to stay as normal as I can for Darby, but it's not working for either one of us." He turned, setting his mug on the counter, his hand going to his abdomen. "Have you talked to Barnabas?"

"Just briefly. The detective was quite interested in that material. He's going to have his techs go over it and then hand it off to one of the detectives helping on the case. They want this solved, Baird."

Baird swayed for a moment, then his eyes closed, his body sagged and he crumpled to the floor as his knees gave way, an arm wrapped around his abdomen, just missing the handle on the oven door, taking the towel hanging there down with him.

Benen was on his knees, his hands rolling Baird to his back, even as he shouted for Darby.

"Darby!" When he heard no response, he yelled again. "Darby! Now! I need your help!"

Darby appeared in the doorway, hair sticking up, eyes half closed against the light, rubbing at his face. "Benen? What's up? Why are you yelling for me?"

"Call for help. Baird just collapsed."

Those words had Darby awake and alert, reaching for the phone on the counter, dialling for emergency services. He stood back, beside Benen, and watched as the paramedics worked on Baird before he was bundled onto a stretcher and then wheeled away.

"Go on. Get dressed, Darby. I'll take you after him."

Darby ran for his room and then ran for the door, Benen after him, watching as Darby slammed the door, lock in place. Benen smiled to himself, noting that Darby seemed to have grabbed the first pieces of clothing he had laid his hands on, not caring about style at all.

Darby sat once more in the surgical waiting room, his foot bobbing up and down with his stress, his eyes on the entrance door, willing the surgeon to come, but afraid to have him come. Buckley sat beside him, his arm around Darby's shoulders. Anna sat on his other side, his hand tight in hers. As many of the other men who could be there, were. Doc had sent word he'd come as soon as his shift finished at the clinic in the shelter downtown.

Darby was on his feet as he saw the same surgeon approaching.

"Doctor? Baird?"

"He's alive, but he wouldn't be if he had been on his own. He was bleeding internally, likely had been all day. What was he doing?"

"Moving around too much, likely." Buckley spoke up. "I'm sure you're aware his wife has been kidnapped, and he is doing everything he can to help find her."

"He needs to rest. He'll not survive another one of these episodes. As it is, right now, it's touch and go. We're sending him to an ICU bed when we can. You, young man, you can see him but only for a bit." The surgeon searched the faces of the men around him. "All of you can in shifts. But I want it understood. He can't continue as he has been. He left too soon the last time. This time, we won't let him go." The surgeon spun on his heel and walked away, anger emanating from his very stride.

"He won't stop. He can't. It will kill him if he has to." Darby's words were quiet but heard by everyone around him. Anna's arm around him kept him close to her.

"We're praying, Darby. We're praying. I'm getting a sense from God that this will end shortly." Anna's words were whispered to the youth.

"I hope so, Anna. Please, God. I pray so." He turned, his head down, unable to control his tears, pushing his way through the men, to drop onto a chair, his head buried against his upraised knees.

Chapter 40

Moving restlessly, Berneen raised her head slightly and rubbed her face against her sleeve, before she rolled to her side from her stomach, her hair flowing around her. She slept again, not moving, the sleep deep and drugged.

The man stood over her, anger on his face. He needed to talk to her, to give her orders as to what she was going to do, but he couldn't. He couldn't get her to wake up. He had no idea how much of the sedative she had been given or how often, but it was wreaking havoc with his plans.

He spun on his heel, slamming through the door and locking it behind him, leaving Berneen enclosed in a windowless room, on her own. He would find the men responsible for this and make them pay. This was not acceptable, he thought, as his heavy footsteps stormed through the house, causing the men there to raise their heads and share a glance. They knew that Berneen had not been given too much sedative but how to explain that to their leader. That was a question none of them wanted to face but they would have no choice, not given the mood he was in.

Berneen stirred again, how much later, she wasn't sure. She dragged her body to a sitting position, pushing her unkempt hair behind her, and then scrubbing at her face, her eyes barely open. She saw the bottle of water beside her and reached for it. Uncapping it, she drank thirstily before she set it back down, her body slumping once more in sleep. She just couldn't stay awake, she thought.

How long she had been like this, she didn't know, awakening again, more alert but still sleepy and not quite aware of what was going on. She sat up, looking around, seeing no windows and only a door. She dragged herself to her feet, stumbling over them as she fell against a wall. Her hands feeling her way along, she searched for a way out, not finding any. She moved more rapidly and more in a panic, finally stopping at the door, her hand clutching at the door knob and shaking it. Her hand still on the knob, she began to strike at the door with her open hand.

"Hey! Open the door! Let me out!" She continued to strike at the door. "Please! Someone? Anyone? Open the door, please? Let me out?"

Her ham fisted, and she began to hammer at the door, finally stepping away as she realized no one heard her, or if they did, that they were not going to open the door as she demanded and let her out. She backed away from the door until she hit the wall opposite it, standing for a moment before she slid to a sitting position on the floor. She shoved her unkempt hair away from her face, scrubbing at her cheeks, feeling the stickiness from the tears she didn't remember shedding. She climbed to her feet once more, heading for the rudimentary sink that stood in a corner, a curtain hiding the toilet from view. She turned the tap cautiously, not sure if there would be water, her eyes sliding closed as water poured from the tap. She scrubbed at her face and hands, not sure if she was getting the dirt and stickiness away from them.

She reached for the thin worn towel that hung there, and then changed her mind. She couldn't use it, not knowing if it had been used by someone before her. She pulled up the sweatshirt she was wearing, using the inside to wipe at the wetness on her face and hands.

That someone else had been held there for a time, she had no doubt. She could see the damage done to the drywall where someone had tried to pry it away from around the door but had been unsuccessful. She had no idea who had taken her. All she could remember was seeing Baird drop to the floor, his hand on his abdomen, and then trying to run, before she was stopped. She rubbed at her arm where she had felt the prick of a needle before her consciousness had fled.

She slumped back to the floor, this time in a corner of the wall that contained the door, her legs out in front of her, ankles crossed, as she wrapped her arms around herself, her thoughts going to the man who had appeared with Barnabas. She knew the name he had given wasn't right but she couldn't place where she had seen him.

Then, as she sorted through her memories, a tiny thought tickled at her memories and then grew. Her eyes shut as she concentrated, then flew open at the memory that surfaced. She groaned. She knew the man, and it wasn't from a pleasant experience. She remembered her father telling her to avoid any contact with him if she could and if she couldn't, then to find him. He would protect her.

She shuddered at her memory. He had approached her one day as she had stood in the local bookstore, his hand clenching her arm in a tight grip as he demanded she call her father. He wanted to speak with him, and her father had been avoiding his calls. She had stared at him, panic setting in, as she jerked at her arm, finally freeing herself as a saleswoman approached them and his grip loosened. She had fled from the store, wanting to find her father, and then realizing he had just left on his trip with her mother. She had hidden herself in the house, making Darby stay inside, much to his dismay. He had protested loud and long, she remembered.

Her head back on the way, her mind drifted. Why, Lord? She questioned Him. Why me? Why this? Who is doing this? I thought that being a Christian meant safety, peace, happiness, joy, protection. This certainly doesn't feel like this. I don't know that I can trust, not like Your Word says I need to. I feel isolated, alone, forgotten. I doubt I'll make it out of here alive. So, where is Your protection? Where are You? How can I trust? My husband is likely dead. I don't know what has happened to my brother. So, tell me, how do I trust You?

Chapter 41

Berneen didn't stir or look up as the door finally opened, and the man walked in, looking for her, stopping just short of her feet. She studied the shoes, the shiny black patent leather, the pointed toes, the dark socks showing just a bit below the creased black dress pants. She didn't respond as he stood there, a foot starting to tap as her refusal to look up.

"Look at me!" The words came out in a staccato manner, harshness behind them, a coarseness she recognized from years gone by. "I said, look at me!"

She refused to look up, even when his hand reached out and clutched her hair at the scalp, pulling backwards, making her face turn up. She kept her eyes down, not wanting to see the cruelty in the face she feared.

"I said, look at me!" Her chin was then grasped and her head tilted further up, her eyes closing.

The man finally stepped back, knowing that for now, she would not obey him. "You will look at me at some point, young lady. If you don't, you'll never go back to your family." He cackled out a cruel laugh. "Those that are still living, that is."

She shuddered at the thought of someone else she loved dying, but she just could not look up. Lord? Is this where I'm supposed to trust You? That You will bring me to safety? Just how do I do that?

She heard his heavy footsteps walk across the floor and out the door, the door slamming behind him, the lock clicking into place.

Now what, she thought? Where do I go from here? He wants something from me, or he wants me to do something for him. That's definitely not an option.

She rose, pacing the room, trying to think of a way to escape, to get away. She turned the door knob, shaking it slightly, finding it locked. She searched for hinges, not seeing them on the inside of the door. Well, she thought, there goes that idea. I can't remove the hinge pins, even if I had something to work with.

She paced more, finally dropping down into the same corner, this time her knees drawn up, her arms folded on them, her chin on her arms. Lord? Where are You? This isn't supposed to happen to Christians, you know. We're supposed to be safe. Or is that what You want me to learn? That no matter where I go, I'm not safe. That's a frightening thought, that I can't be safe anywhere. Mom and Dad sure weren't.

She paused as she thought about that, wondering who had been responsible for their deaths. Her eyes slanted towards the door, knowing that the man who had left her here was likely responsible in some way. She shuddered at the thought.

Her head rested against the wall and she slept, not hearing the door unlock again and lighter footsteps approach her, setting down a tray on the floor beside her, before the man stepped back, his eyes on her, a look on his face that said he would do his best to get her out of there. He was low man on the totem pole, he thought. He didn't realize he had signed on for this. He didn't like it, not one bit.

He walked away, locking the door, but not wanting to do that. He had no choice. The boss expected the key to be returned to him, and the younger man knew he would check the door himself.

Berneen eventually roused, not sure what had awakened her. She stood, feeling the floor shaking under her. She spun, her eyes huge with fear, then ran for the door, shaking at the knob, pounding on the door, unable to elicit any response. She felt the building shaking and she spun once more, unable to escape, not knowing what was happening, fear coursing through her body in a deeper and deeper wave. She headed for a corner, not sure if she would even be safe there. Then, the floor gave way beneath her, and she fell the few feet to the crawlspace under the floor, her head hitting against the flooring and her eyes closed as her body sagged and went limp, her head dropping back against the floor. She didn't hear the yells of the men as they ran for safety, leaving her the only occupant of the now shaky, almost demolished building. They didn't know that this had been planned, that they were to have died along with Berneen, when the building collapsed, and that for some reason, the building didn't collapse all the way, allowing their escape, and allowing a small space that kept Berneen safe.

Chapter 42

Red and blue emergency vehicle lights played across the scene, highlighting the fragility and instability of the building as men and women milled around, shouts and answers ringing through the air.

Barnabas stood for a moment, staring at the building, then down at a paper in his hand, his heart falling as he realized that he stood in front of the building that they had tracked Berneen to. Was he too late? Had she escaped? He looked around, finding the fire captain walking towards him.

"Ron?"

"Barnabas? What are you doing here?" Ron Walker turned to face the building. "We're looking but we don't think anyone was inside."

"I think there was." Barnabas' voice was barely audible.

"What?" Ron spun back to face him. "Whatever do you mean?"

"I mean this." He held up the piece of paper. "We tracked Baird's wife to here. We think she was held captive here. Oh, God! Please! Don't let her be dead!" Barnabas cry went to the heart of the man standing beside him.

"How sure are you?" Ron took the paper Barnabas held out to him and read it. "You're sure?"

"As sure as we can be." He looked around, seeing Brady walking towards him. "And now I have to tell a friend she's in there."

"Barnabas?" Brady's voice held a question. "Why are you here?" His voice died away as he began to shake his head and turned to the building. "No! She's not, is she?"

"Benen and Burney tracked her to here. I don't know how, but they did."

Brady stared at him and then turned to the fire captain. "Captain? Can we search?"

"No, it's not stable enough." He walked away, his arm waving at some of his men, who ran towards him and then ran towards the engine, pulling equipment from it.

"They'll search, Brady, from outside. That looks like a heat sensing camera." Barnabas had followed Ron to where he was sending his men to searching.

"It is, Barnabas. Pray that if she's in there, we can find her and that she's in a spot we can access." Ron looked up at the building. "Pete. Call for a crane. Have it ready to move in when I say."

Hours passed. Brady sat on the step of his paramedic rig, the light from the huge spotlights reflecting from the stripes on his uniform. Barnabas had been back and forth, returning this time with Buckley, Bradon and Breck. Bradon had Kade with him, just in case he said. He didn't elaborate but they knew what he was referring to and their hearts sank.

Their prayer was to find Berneen alive and that they could get to her.

A sudden shout had all heads turning towards the back corner of the house and Brady was on his feet, running that way.

"Captain?" His question was almost breathless, he was so afraid of what he would hear.

"We have a heat source here, Brady." Ron moved his men away. "The crane will stabilize the building enough so that I can send someone in."

"Me." He stared at the captain. "Please sir. Let me go."

Ron finally nodded. "Okay. Get yourself geared up as you need to. I want someone to go with you."

"It's a crawl space, Captain. There won't be room for more than me, I suspect." Brady ran for the rig and then was back, ready to enter through a shattered window when he was given word. A heavy tarp dropped to the ground at his feet, ready to cover the window frame.

Barnabas stood as close as he was allowed, the three other men nearby as they watched Brady speaking with the captain before, with a clap of the older man's hand to his shoulder, he picked up the tarp and headed for the window. The four friends exchanged glances, knowing they were praying that it was Berneen who had been spotted and that she was alive now. It had seemed like hours since the heat source was found.

Brady draped the tarp over the window frame, pausing to pray for a moment, before he slid feet first into the crawl space, the light from the torch he held shining eerily around. He could hear the drip from pipes that still held a bit of water. He knew the utilities had been shut off, so that wasn't a concern. He just didn't know how clear a path he would have to where the person was. He prayed it was Berneen, not someone else. They needed to find her for Baird. Baird was still being kept unconscious, the surgeon concerned about the bleeding.

He moved forward, his gloved hands feeling his way, until he felt a small object in his way and stopped, digging through the sand and dirt, uncovering match-box sized tin boxes, five of them. He frowned for a moment as he studied them, then scooped them up, sticking them into a pocket on his uniform cargo pants and zipping the pocket closed before he shone the light around. A foot showed briefly as he flashed the light by it and then he trained the light on the foot, playing it around, seeing the body lying there, almost lifeless, he thought.

He crept forward, hearing the groaning and squeaking of the building, knowing that at any moment it could give way. The crane had support chains and ropes running to the building, but that didn't help inside. He reached for the foot, feeling how small it was, and knew it was a woman. He crept closely, not minding the stones and debris he was crawling over, not seeing the dust and bits of debris dropping into his line of sight, ducking below the jagged edges of the wood. He felt for the arm, found the wrist and with a quick motion, had his glove off feeling for a pulse. His head dropped briefly. She was alive.

He moved carefully to edge her nearer him, mindful that she could have injuries he would worsen by that very activity, but he had no choice. He had to do this. There wasn't room for a backboard or neck collar. He paused for a moment and then with a sigh, reached for the scissors in his other pants pocket, reaching to carefully cut away the hair that was trapped under a beam, hurting for her with each strand his scissors sliced through.

He worked his way carefully backwards towards the window, his movements gentle, his eyes on the woman's face until he could see it. Thank you, God, he thought. It's Berneen. She's alive. Please, hold up the building until we're out. That's all I'm asking right now.

He moved back until he was at the window and saw the men, the captain among them, watching for him. Eager hands reached to take Berneen from him as he gently lifted her up and through the window, to be placed carefully on a backboard and then rushed to the waiting stretcher. Brady reached for the hands and arms that pulled him through the window and once on his feet, ran for Berneen, wanting to be the one who took her in for treatment. The captain nodded, his eyes raising to where Barnabas and the others waited.

The captain walked towards them. "We have her, Barnabas. She's alive." He watched with compassion as the men's faces relaxed and almost tears clouded their eyes.

———

"How is she?" Barnabas could barely get the words out. He had not known Berneen long he thought, but she had become an important part of their lives, just because of Baird.

"I don't know. She's unconscious. Brady didn't say much when he handed off to us, other than to be careful." Ron turned, his eyes on the paramedics as they were loading the stretcher. "Head off with them, Barnabas. Stay right behind the rig. I'm sending an escort with you. The police chief has authorized it.

A sudden yell had them all turning, watching both in fascination and horror as the building shuddered and then collapsed on itself, tearing away the restraints from the crane. The four friends stood in shock, realizing how close it had been for Berneen and Brady not making it out.

Chapter 43

His feet sounded quietly on the tiled floor, Barnabas headed for the ICU rooms, Buckley keeping step with him. They needed to find Darby and knew he would be around that area somewhere.

"Did Brady give any hint as to her condition when you talked to him, Buckley?"

Buckley shook his head. "Not really, other than she was likely dehydrated and unconscious. He asked that we pray it's not serious."

"That we can." Barnabas paused at the entrance to the chapel, peeking through the doors, seeing Anna there. "Anna's in there. She needs to go home."

"She won't. Not while her boys, as she calls them, need her. And now that Berneen is here? She definitely won't. She always wanted a daughter, but only had sons. She has quite taken to Berneen."

"That she has. I'm glad for Berneen's sake. She needs her." Barnabas sighed as they walked towards the waiting room, finding Darby huddled in the corner, his eyes on the door to the rooms. "He just won't leave."

"No, he won't. Not until Baird can tell him to. And that's not happening any day soon." Buckley paused, his thoughts muddled for a moment. "The church has had the prayer chain working every day, all day, and the board members and trustees have kept the church open."

"That helps."

Even though it was late at night, Darby was making no effort to leave. He couldn't, he told them. He needed to be with Baird. He didn't look up as the two men sat on either side of him.

Barnabas' arm came out around Darby's shoulders, knowing that when he spoke, Darby would be on his feet, running for the Emergency Department, and they needed to prepare him, for what he would see when he found his sister.

"Darby?" When the youth didn't respond, Barnabas shared a looked with Buckley. "Darby, I need you to listen to me."

Darby looked around, a bleak look on his face, fatigue showing, his face white. "What is it, Barnabas? More bad news about Baird."

"There has been news?"

Darby nodded. "They took him back to surgery a bit ago. There was an area the surgeon was concerned about. They're talking about needing to transfuse him, I think they said."

"No, I hadn't heard. Was someone with you when they talked to you?"

Darby nodded. "Doc and Anna. Branigan was here as well." He sighed, his eye closing as he fought his tears and lost the battle.

"Okay. So we pray harder. But that's not what I wanted to talk to you about." Barnabas' voice was gentle, but Darby's head shot around and he stared at him.

"No! Please, God. No! She can't be gone!"

"Whoa, there, Darby. She's not. We found her but she is hurt. She's downstairs right now being looked after." His arm tightened on Darby as Darby made a move to rise. "Wait, please. We need to tell you what happened." He went on to explain how they had tracked Berneen to the house, only to find the house was collapsing, that they had searched and found her, Brady going in to bring her out. He looked up at that point to see Brady approaching, staring down at something in his hands.

Darby looked up and then was on his feet away from the two men, almost running towards Brady. "Brady? Thank you." He hugged Brady, his arms tight before he stepped back. "Can I go to her? Can I see her?"

"You can. I'll take you down in just a moment. First, I need to give these to Barnabas."

"What are those?" Darby peered closer. "They look like old match tins."

"That's what they are. They have something in that that I can't get out. We'll figure it out." He handed them to Barnabas. "I found them before I found Berneen."

Barnabas studied them, feeling the weight of an object inside each one, before he dropped them into a pocket. "We'll look at them. Right now, Darby needs his sister."

Brady nodded, as hand on Darby's shoulder, he turned him and walked him back to the elevator, not knowing or caring how dirty his uniform had become during his crawl under the house.

Darby stood at his sister's bedside, watching as her head turned slightly in a restless manner. He saw the bruise on her forehead and winced. He hadn't spoken to the doctor yet although he could hear him talking to a nurse outside the curtain. He was just thankful his sister was back with him.

Chapter 44

Sore, battered, tired, her mind still foggy, fighting a headache, but showered and in clean clothes, Berneen stood at Baird's bedside, her hand resting against his cheek, seeing the hollows that had appeared in them. She felt the stubble that she knew he would not like. How she knew that, she wasn't sure. It was just something she knew.

She watched as he slept, the intubation tube still in place, IVs running to his arms, the heart monitor leads. She knew he had had a blood transfusion and knew just who had given his blood. She would need to find Doc at some point and thank him.

She had heard about his three surgeries, her heart breaking for him, knowing that even now, he was still in danger. She had been told that bluntly by the surgeon. In fact, she was told Baird should not be alive. The surgeon had no idea why he was. Berneen had given a small smile at that, knowing exactly Who had kept him alive.

She had talked at length with the detective, letting him know who had abducted her and how she knew him. She told him how terrified of the man she was, given his actions in the past. She now had a police officer assigned to her all the time. It was a given, she was told, that the man would make another try for her.

She had had no words to thank Brady, just gave him a long hug, for his part in rescuing her. He had just nodded, dropped a kiss on her cheek, and said you're welcome. He had not wanted her thanks, that she knew. She understood just how much of a risk he had taken, but he had said it was all part of his job. She knew better. She had been told he had been the one to volunteer to go in, not wanting anyone else to risk their lives for her.

Darby wouldn't move from her side, desperate to make sure she kept safe. He had told her that he had been so afraid she wouldn't come back, that he couldn't handle losing anyone else in his family. His eyes had strayed to Baird at that point, and Berneen understood without words how worried he was and just how much Baird had come to mean to him.

She heard the nurse's footsteps coming towards her and looked up at the clock. Her time was up for now. She reached to kiss Baird's cheek, a whispered I love you to his ear, and then stood back, wiping at the tears on her face before she turned and headed for the waiting room.

She had sent Darby home to sleep, Branigan staying with him. She had objected, but Branigan had just shrugged, saying this was what they did. Their employers gave them that flexibility. Because Barnabas was the one who paid them and if he didn't object, how could they?

She slumped into a chair, reaching for a blanket to wrap around herself. A bottle of water appeared in her line of sight and she took it with a word of thanks. Buckley seated himself beside her, his eyes watchful.

"How is Baird?"

"The same, I think, Buckley. They still don't know if he'll rouse or not." Her head went back against the wall behind her, and she pulled at her hair. "Brady felt so bad."

"About what?"

"That he had to cut my hair to free me. I don't care. Hair will grow. He can't feel guilty."

Buckley gave a small laugh. "Then you don't know?"

"Know what?" Her head twisted to watch him.

"That Baird loves your long hair. He made some comment to Brady just after you two were married, something along the lines that he hoped you never cut it."

"I didn't know that."

"There are a lot of things you two need to talk about. That is one of them." Buckley sighed. "It shouldn't have happened how it did."

"But you said God allowed it, didn't you? So how can we doubt? I had a lot of time to think this last time. I got mad at God, told Him off, yelled at Him." She looked shamefaced as she said this.

"I think at times we all feel something like that. It's all part of growing as His child. It's part of learning to trust." He gave her a long look. "And that is something you've been dealing with."

"It is, Buckley. It's been so hard to trust, for the last ten years. I have wanted my parents, needed them, and had no one I could turn to."

"We get that, Berneen. We get that Darby feels the same. You two need to talk at some point." He turned his head as he heard rubber-soled footsteps heading their way and was on his feet as a nurse hurriedly approached.

"Mrs. Cassidy, can you come with me? The surgeon needs to speak with you."

Berneen's face whitened and she reached for Buckley's hand, not letting go until she stood in Baird's room, her eyes on the surgeon before flickering to Baird, a frown coming on her face as she saw the intubation tube gone.

"Doctor?"

"Mrs. Cassidy, if I had been a betting man, I would have said your husband would be gone by now. Instead, he is breathing room air with the help of oxygen by nasal prongs. We've begun the process of weaning him off the medications. All the imaging done today is clear, not like yesterday that still showed a huge area of concern." He stared at her before looking at Buckley. "So you tell me, why?"

"God. Plain and simple, Doctor. God." Buckley spoke for them.

"You almost make me believe."

"Believe, Doctor. You have been part of a miracle." Berneen moved away to stand at Baird's side, her hand on his cheek, her other hand holding his, feeling his fingers close around her, even as his eyes flickered open and a small smile creased his face, before he dropped off into a normal, natural sleep.

———

Chapter 45

Berneen stood, hands on her hips, watching in frustration as Baird moved slowly around his office in the apartment a week later. She wanted him to rest, to lie down, or at least sit down, and he was refusing. He needed to work, he said. She argued with him, finally throwing up her hands in defeat and turning to walk away from him. She didn't hear the soft sound of his socked feet approaching her until his arms came around her.

"I heard you, Berneen. That's what brought me back. I was almost Home, I think. I could see the light of heaven. But your voice and your words brought me back to you." His head rested against her. "I love you, too. I didn't want to live if you weren't here. I couldn't go on."

She stood still, listening to him, before her hands were raised to grip his. "I know, Baird. I know. I didn't think I could live either. I was sure you were dead. You went down so fast and there was so much blood."

"Can you live here still? Given what happened? Barnabas has had it all repainted, new flooring, new window treatments. He said he will change anything you don't like. Or if you can't live here, he'll move us to another apartment."

She turned then, her arms around him, being mindful of the hurt and incision area. "I can. As long as you are here, I can. Can you?"

He shrugged. "I can live wherever you are. We need to talk over things, we need to talk to Darby too, but that can wait."

She nodded before she moved away, heading for the kitchen. She had put on coffee for him and was determined to get him to sit somehow. He needed to. She had been warned to have him rest as much as she could.

She frowned as she heard a tap at the door, glancing down the hallway at Baird as he approached, his hand on his abdomen, a frown on his face.

"Were we expecting anyone?" His voice was quiet.

"No, not that I am aware of. Darby's off with some of the guys, hiking some of the Bruce Trail. Barnabas said he had put out the word that you needed to rest and no one was to come near you. Unless it's Doc or Anna."

She gave a scream as a hard kick at the door broke the lock and sent the door flying to crash against an inside wall. She stared at the sledge hammer held by the man who entered and realized it had been that he had used to break in. She backed away, backed into Baird, whose arms encircled her, even as he spoke.

"Who are you?"

"You're coming with us."

"I don't think so." Baird simply shook his head, his arms tight around Berneen. "We're not going anywhere."

"Oh, I think you are." The man raised the sledge hammer, bringing it down on the hallway wall, leaving a huge hole in the drywall. "This says you do."

"And this says they don't." Branigan stood there, a weapon to the man's neck. "Drop it! I said, drop it!"

The man finally dropped the sledge hammer, his eyes burning with hatred at Baird and Berneen.

Branigan shoved the man at the officer who was just entering. "He's wanted, I think, on multiple charges, including abduction, attempted abduction, assault, breaking and entering, just for starters."

Berneen stared at him for a moment. "How did you know?"

Branigan shrugged. "I was coming to see how you were and heard the commotion." He shared a look with Baird, shaking his head slightly.

Baird nodded, knowing they would talk later.

"Well, now that he's gone, coffee anyone?" Berneen moved to the kitchen, reaching for mugs, pouring the men their coffee, reaching for her tea and realizing she didn't want that anymore. Her mug in her hand when Baird was hurt had turned her off her tea.

"Berneen? Your tea?" Baird's arm came around her.

“I can’t, Baird. I need to find something else.” She swiped his mug of coffee, sipping at it. “This isn’t so bad after all.”

She slid into a seat at the table, leaving him staring openmouthed at her, as Branigan rubbed at his upper lip, trying to hide a grin.

“So, Branigan, what else was it you wanted?” She smirked as he laughed, Baird’s comment that she should know better than to ask that ringing in her ears.

Chapter 46

Walking through the church parking lot after church the following Sunday, Berneen felt content, her hand in Baird's, knowing just how much they had been prayed for. She was thankful. She had found that God was faithful. She was learning to trust. To trust God in a way she had never thought she could. Learning to trust Baird. Learning to trust his friends, who counted her as a sister now. Learning to trust Darby. Learning also that she had to leave everything in God's hands.

Baird had watched Berneen's face during the service, seeing the peace and contentment that was beginning to show. He knew the men were still out there, that they had been spotted in the area, but that they had so far eluded arrest. That worried him, and that worry he was learning to leave with God.

Darby had run ahead of them, eager to be home. Baird had promised to show him some plans for tutoring that he was working on, and that was something Darby was interested in. He had energy to burn he thought, and hoped one of the men would be willing to run the beach near their home today. They quite often did that.

He slid to a halt, his hands rising as he saw the man appear from behind the car, a weapon pointed at Darby's head. He motioned Darby closer and when Darby didn't move, the man stalked towards him, roughly grabbing him by the arm before he spun him around and snaked his arm around Darby's neck, the weapon muzzle digging into Darby's temple. Darby froze, not sure what he should be doing or what the man wanted. He hadn't said and Darby was too afraid to ask.

Baird stopped suddenly, his eyes on Darby, causing Berneen to frown up at him, her words dying on her lips as she followed his line of sight. She paled, moved to run towards him, and was only stopped by Baird's arm around her. That caused him pain, but he didn't care. He needed Berneen to stay safe and somehow they needed to free Darby.

"What do you want?" Baird voice echoed through the stillness that ensued when onlookers realized what was happening.

"You know what I want. That thumb drive."

"We don't have it. We can't get it." Baird was playing for time, watching Bradon move around behind the car, Kade by his side, alert, ready to attack when he was given the order. That couldn't happen, not yet.

Berneen dropped to the ground, her hands covering her mouth, not sure what was going on.

"That's him, Baird. That's the man who held me captive. Each time. I recognize his voice." She paused. "But I know it from when I was a teen. He's the man who tried to snatch me when Mom and Dad were still alive. But there's someone else."

"That's right, little lady. There is someone else. And he's behind you." The man moved his weapon enough to gesture with it. That was all Kade needed.

225

Without warning and with only a slight movement of Bradon's hand, he was moving, flying over the car, the man's arm in his grip as he took him down, Darby rolling away, hands reaching for him to pull him to safety.

Baird dove for Berneen, driving her down, a groan coming from him even as he covered her body with his. She shivered from fear, hearing the calls and shouts, then felt the hands on her, raising her to her feet. She stopped, her eyes on Baird even as she flung herself into his arms, hers tight around him.

"You're okay? You didn't get hurt again?"

"I'm okay. It hurts but that's okay. You're okay?" Baird leaned back, studying the face of the woman he knew he loved beyond anything he thought possible. "You're okay, Sweetheart. I love you." He kissed her, then heard a throat clearing beside him. "Go away, Barnabas. Let me kiss my best girl."

"That's fine. You can do that. But I have a young man here who needs his sister."

Berneen struggled to release herself from Baird's grip, her eyes on her brother before she had him in a tight hug. She felt his tears on her face, knowing they mixed with hers. She looked around at Baird finally, not having noticed his arms surround them both.

"Is it over, Baird?"

"It is, Sweetheart. Barnabas tells me that the man behind it all was standing back of us. He was ready to shoot us."

She shuddered once more. "I'm glad. Can we just go home now, please?"

He laughed, even as his arms tightened around the two he held. "We can. We'll find out what it's all about later."

Chapter 47

Holding his mug of coffee, Barnabas leaned against a table in the building conference room, a smile on his face as he listened the conversation, the laughter, the teasing and feeling the relief that it was all over for Baird. The men and women, yes, women, he thought, were all in custody. The authorities were still sorting through everything but he had been told enough so that he could share with his men, Doc and Anna, and Baird, Berneen and Darby. It was only fair, he thought. All of them had been through a lot in such a short period of time.

"They're doing okay, Baird and Berneen."

"They are, all things considered. Darby's had to grow up faster than he should have, given what has happened in his life." Barnabas sipped at his mug of coffee before he set it behind him on the table. "Now, if I can get their attention, I can let them know what was going on and why."

"You start at this side of the room. I'll do the other." Breck moved away, a quiet word spoken to each man, watching at Barnabas did the same, before his friend halted beside Berneen, a comment from him making her laugh.

Barnabas studied each man in front of him, praying that none of the rest would go through what Baird had done, but knowing in his heart what likely faced all of them.

"I spoke with the detective earlier today. This meal that Anna and Doc has provided for us is the right time and right opportunity to tell you what was going on.

"Baird, your father had been called in on that job site. He found major issues in the design. The building was brought down around them. The authorities have been trying for years to find the men responsible, and couldn't until now. It is up to the courts what they face. I'm sorry. I wish I could have said it was an accident but it wasn't.

"Berneen, Darby. Your parents were sent overseas on that trip. Your mother was not to have gone but the woman who arranged it insisted that she go. Your father provided a wealth of information on that thumb drive. He also provided the information in those little boxes Brady found the day he rescued you. We don't know why they were there. Only God does. But suffice it to say there was enough information there for the authorities to bring down a group who had been plaguing the city with numerous bad builds. These people no one could or would name. He did that. We have been told that is why he was sent overseas. Their thinking was that if he was involved in a riot overseas and killed, no one would question it. You did. A word from you was all it took to set the men after you.

"The man at the head of it, Tom Paul, had a grudge against both your fathers. He set them up for murder. He also had his brother killed. He's the one who was here that day. We didn't realize it in time, he didn't give us an opportunity to do that.

"The building you were held in? It belonged to a numbered company traced back to him. We have experts examining it but it had been damaged in a way that would bring it down. He thought you would die in it and that would be the end of it.

"Darby. Berneen. Baird. The authorities have asked that I extend their thanks to you three. You have helped bringdown a group of men and women they have been after for years. Your courage and faith have spoken loudly to them. There will be court to face but we'll have the lawyers that you need."

Barnabas stopped speaking for a moment, unable to continue. He looked around at the other men.

"My thanks to each one of you, guys. This is what friendship is. This is what we do. You have all been an encouragement to each other, in many ways and forms."

Baird finally spoke. "That place Berneen was kept in at first. Why?"

"One of the men said that it was to break her spirit and bring her down. They had plans for her but when they saw you that day and had heard you would be in the area, the plans changed. They saw an opportunity to seek revenge. The plan all along for you two was what they forced on you. Marriage. Then the death of one or the other of you. It didn't matter to them which one. The men Berneen saw before you, Baird? It was what was suspected. They were men from the gang, made up to look as if they had been beaten. That was all part of wearing her down. It didn't seem to work."

He looked over at Doc and Anna. "Doc. Anna. I know your prayers were there, helping get us through. Thank you." He walked away, his hands stuffed into his pockets, not speaking, leaving quiet murmurs behind him.

Epilogue

Baird was on a search. He couldn't find Berneen anywhere. It had been three weeks since Barnabas had talked to them. He needs to see her, to talk to her. He searched through the apartment and then headed for his office, walking better than he had, the pain in his abdomen lessening each day.

Darby just smirked when he was asked where Berneen was. "Lose your wife already, Baird?"

Baird stared at him, laughed and then hugged the youth he thought of as a brother. "No. She's just good at hiding."

He finally walked from the building a frown on his face, before Bradon took pity on him.

"Try the beach. She likes to walk there."

"She does? I didn't know that."

"She heads there every day at some point. You need to learn what your wife does, Baird." Bradon ducked the playful swat Baird aimed his way before he headed for the path to the beach.

Baird stopped, leaning against a rock pile, his eyes on Berneen as she stood, arms wrapped around herself, her hair flying loose around her face. He didn't know if he liked her hair better loose or in the braid she wore most days.

———

He finally walked through the sand, his arms reaching to encircle her and pull her back against him, content just to stand and watch the waves beating against the shore, even though the wind was cold.

He finally spoke. "Ready to go home, Sweetheart?"

"I am, Baird, my love. I am. We can finally get on with our lives, can't we?"

"We can. And you are staying with me, aren't you?" A little bit of fear and uncertainty came through.

She turned, her face raised to study him. "I am. I wasn't sure if that's what you wanted. I know it's what I want."

He bent to kiss her, then studied her face. "It's what I want. I used to wonder why my wife would look like, I mean, hair colour, eyes, height. You are more than what I ever imagined."

"I never thought I would ever marry. Not raising Darby. Men would ask me out but when I said I had a little brother to look after, they backed away. You didn't, even if you could have. You just made him part of your family. He needed that. Thank you."

"God has blessed us, Sweetheart. And you are the sweetest part of my heart, did you know that?"

"I am. Thank you, Baird." She stood on tiptoes to kiss him, her arms around his neck in a hard hug. "God is good, Baird. I have learned to trust Him in ways I didn't think I could."

"He does that to you, you know? Makes you trust Him."

———

He turned her to walk back towards the buildings, her hand tight in his, content, knowing that God had protected them through everything. He knew there had been times neither thought they would survive, but they had been encouraged by their friends to keep on trusting. That's what, he thought. That's what got us through. Trusting.

Dear Readers

Thank you for choosing to read the story of Baird and his Berneen. What an adventure they had! Learning to trust along the way! God does that, you know. Brings us to a point where we have to trust and lean only on Him.

Trust has been on my mind a lot in the last few weeks. It was not what I had envisioned for being so strong in this story, but that's how the characters work the plot line. They decide the story, I'm just along for the ride and as a scribe.

During this time, I have taken in a six-year-old Shetland Sheepdog named Summer at the request of her breeder, a good friend of mine. We have been working through trust issues, Summer and I. She has been learning to trust me in so many ways and seeing how she has opened up to me, seeing her tail wag as she greets me, feeling her poke me with her nose. I know the trust has come.

The concept for this series is based on Barnabas, companion to Paul on some of his journeys. Barnabas has always been a favourite of mine. The idea of being an encourager, a Barnabas, has been something I have sought to do throughout my life. Only God knows how successful that has been.

As you journey through life, remember. Trust God. Encourage someone. In encouraging someone, you are encouraged yourself.

God bless

Ronna